VICKI AND THE
BLACK HORSE

Written and Illustrated by
Sam Savitt

SCHOLASTIC BOOK SERVICES
New York Toronto London Auckland Sydney Tokyo

For
MATILDA ORKIN
with love

ISBN: 0-590-10159-5

Copyright © 1964 by Sam Savitt. This edition is published by
Scholastic Book Services, a division of Scholastic Magazines, Inc.,
by arrangement with Doubleday & Company, Inc.

13 12 11 10 9 8 7 6 5   1/8

Printed in the U.S.A.

Contents

1. Trapped

The wind was edged with ice. It was blowing from the northwest and struck Vicki Jordan full blast when she stepped down from the school bus in front of her house. She hunched forward, hugging her books against her chest, as she scrambled up the slippery drive. Rocky, her Irish setter, met her halfway, then bounded ahead through the banked snow. He was waiting at the door when she got there and scooted inside when she opened it. She roughed up his grinning face, kicked loose her boots in the hallway, and without taking off her parka made a beeline for the kitchen and the cookie jar on the second shelf above the counter.

Her quick eye immediately caught the note on the kitchen table, and while she munched her cookie she read: "Dear Vicki, Pat is turned out. Bring him in when you feed the animals. Wayne is at basketball practice and I'll be home at six. Love, Mom."

It was four-fifteen. It would start getting dark in about twenty minutes — so she had better get going.

The thermometer outside the window read eighteen degrees above zero, but as she trudged down to the barn it felt more like eighteen below. Snow was starting to fall again. The gray sky had darkened and a thin film of blowing white was beginning to fog the woods along the pasture.

The ducks, with their heads tucked under their wings, looked like a pile of snowballs huddled together in one corner of their pen. Why in the world didn't they get inside their house like Teddy, her goat, who didn't even bother to stick his head out as she went by. Gee it was cold!

By comparison, the inside of the barn seemed warm. The stall door was open. Poor Pat, Vicki thought, out on a day like this. But he has to stretch the kinks out of his muscles even if it's too cold for anyone to ride him.

She plugged in the water heater, then cleaned out the stall and fluffed up the soft dry shavings with a rake. She would bring Pat in as soon as she got his dinner mixed. He would love a hot mash tonight — bran and oats and molasses and hot water made the most delicious-smelling concoction. She had even tasted it once.

Just thinking about Pat made her green eyes grow misty and the rest of her glow all over. Her best friend Kathy had told her that was the way it felt to be in love. But Vicki said she wouldn't know about that, considering how little she thought about boys.

To have a horse like Pat to take care of made her the luckiest girl in the eighth grade. He was sleek and black, with one white star on his forehead. He was her dad's horse, but Vicki had been wishing he belonged to her from the first day he came to Random Farm. He was sick then with a horrible cough, but Dan Jordan had patiently nursed him along with special feed and Vicki's untiring help. She used to walk him slowly along the dirt road that ran for miles from their barnyard through some of the most beautiful countryside in Westchester County. Each time he choked up she would stop him, put her face against his warm neck and wince as cough after cough racked his thin body. Dr. Regan, the veterinarian, was a frequent visitor, and after long months Pat began to get well.

Vicki used to think he had more ribs than any horse she had ever seen, but as he recovered they faded, and his taut hide was replaced by a coat that shone like black satin. His neck filled out and arched into alert ears and a fine Thoroughbred head. When his breathing eased, his step came alive and Vicki knew then that he was the most beautiful, kindest, sweetest, most wonderful horse she had ever known. She had heard that patients sometimes fell in love with their nurses. Perhaps that was what had happened to Pat, for he seemed to return the deep love she felt for him.

When she shouted, "Hey, Black Horse!" he would come galloping up to her as if to run her down, but he would always pull up in the nick of time — then reach out and nuzzle her with his velvet lips — almost knocking her down. His chin always seemed to be itchy and he liked to use the top of her head for a scratching post.

Now she dumped the mash into his feed bucket. She stepped outside and around the corner of the barn, cupped her mittened hand around her mouth, and shouted, "Hey, Black Horse, come and get it!"

In the driving wind her words were lost. It had begun to snow harder. The drifts were thigh-deep here but she could still make out Pat's tracks, and used them as a pathway as she trudged toward the pasture fence.

Pat was nowhere to be seen. She called again and again. Maybe there was an answering whinny — but she couldn't be sure.

As yet she felt no real alarm, only an odd tightening in her throat and quivering in her stomach. "Pat, hey Pat — Pat!" A cold chill settled between her shoulder blades and began to creep up the back of her neck. She ducked under the barway, then floundered along the rail fence to the upper pasture where she hoped he would be. He *had* to be there.

He *was* there — standing like a statue facing the wind. Her first reaction was relief. But why wasn't his back to the wind and why was he so still, with the icy blast slashing against his chest? His head was low, watching her weaving approach. The black mane was flying about, torn by the sharp gusts of wind. As she came closer, she could see the frost collecting around his muzzle and his dark eyes blinking against the sharp sting of snow.

"Pat, why don't you come — "

Then she *saw* the answer. Pat was trapped — in barbed

wire! Wire that had gone unnoticed, buried in the deep snow these many winter months. Now it reached up and held the horse in its twisted strands. Suddenly she remembered all the terrifying stories of horses caught in wire — stories of horses who became ensnarled this way and fought for their freedom until they died from loss of blood and exhaustion. Caught like this, some horses would have panicked and practically committed suicide.

Only last month one of the McLean's prize hunters got tangled up in barbed wire so badly he had to be destroyed. And the Watkins' mare, Loli, just across the way, had been seriously cut up by wire six months ago, and wasn't sound yet.

And now Pat, her beloved Pat, was in the same nightmare situation. If only she could wake up in a minute to find it was just a bad dream. But it was no dream! Her first thought was to call out for help. But then she remembered no one was home.

All this flashed through her mind in the space of a heartbeat. She turned and stumbled down the back trail. She no longer felt the cold or the buffeting wind. "The wire cutters," she thought, "I've got to get the wire cutters." She found them where her dad always hung them, next to the hay chute.

Darkness was beginning to fall — blending with the storm.

"Oh, Pat, don't move. Wait for me. Don't panic! Wait for me." He was where she had left him, still standing, but trembling all over. He must have been caught here for hours. The cold was beginning to get to him — and the fear.

Pat was a Thoroughbred — bred to race, and more high-strung than most other breeds. Every instinct within him cried, bolt — fight — run — run! But some vague, outer good sense held him in place.

Vicki's parka hood had blown back and now her short dark hair was whipping wildly against Pat's belly as she crouched down.

The situation looked even worse than she had feared. The old garden used to be here. Last fall Vicki's father had converted it to pasture. He had spent days digging up old fence and rusted wire which had been in the ground for more than twenty years. Vicki and her brother Wayne had helped, and figured they had gotten all of it. How they had overlooked this section she would never know. But Pat, pawing through the snow, had disturbed the remains. Now he stood ensnared, with two heavy strands of tangled wire running between his front and hind legs — parallel to his body and only six inches below it. His feet were immobilized deep in a cobweb of barbed coils. His knees were shaking and beginning to buckle.

Vicki clamped the cutters down on the upper wire and pressed the handles with all her might. Snap — then — ping! The strand parted and the ends recoiled sharply. Pat was startled, but held fast as the loose ends slapped against his legs. Be careful now, she told herself, steady — no quick moves. He is close to the breaking point; almost anything might set him off.

The wire cutters were fastened on the second wire. Vicki grimaced with pain and frustration as the grips dug into the palms of her hands. But the grips wouldn't close — the wire was too thick. She shifted to another spot and tried again. Then she threw the cutters down in the snow and seized the wire in her hands. Back and forth, back and forth. "Break! please break!" she said aloud, gritting her teeth until her jaws ached. The rusty wire turned red under the desperate efforts of her bleeding hands, but she never felt the hurt. Finally the strand gave way with a jerk that threw her down. She was gasping for air. It was bitterly cold but the hair above her eyes was matted with sweat.

Her fingers were numb as she dug down through the snow, frantically searching for the wire around Pat's front feet. She could feel it, wrapped and twisted around his hoofs. She reached for the wire cutters again. On her belly now, the snow almost blinding her, she struggled with the wire. Cut...cut...cut, and Pat was free — but only in front!

Vicki lurched to her feet, dizzy with exhaustion. She held onto his halter for support — her face against his neck.

"Steady Pat," she gasped, "we're almost through — just a little longer.

She pressed gently against his shoulder, pushing sideways. He stepped clear reluctantly, fearfully, still not sure. As he turned, his back legs, still trapped, stayed where they were, but crossed slightly as he pivoted away from them.

"Hold it, you're not clear yet!"

The black horse seemed to understand what she was saying and know that Vicki was trying to help him.

On her knees again, she found the wire behind. There seemed to be no sensation left in her hands. They worked automatically like things apart — on a mission of their own. All that mattered was to get Pat out of this. His complete faith and trust gave her a strength she didn't know she had.

Vicki cut the last strand and dragged it aside. At Pat's head, she led him slowly forward, one step at a time, until he was in the clear. Then she reeled back away from him. Pat reared, then plunged ahead in the exuberance of his freedom. All his pent-up feelings exploded in a series of bucks and kicks as he headed toward the barn. Vicki staggered along behind, but once inside she quickly cross-tied him and carefully examined his legs. There wasn't a mark on him!

It was a miracle. She could hardly believe her eyes. Nobody would believe anything like this could have happened — but it had. The palms of her hands, torn and crusted with blood, and the ripped sleeves of her parka were proof. But Pat, wonderful Pat, was alive and unhurt!

Vicki's father got home late that evening. He had been detained at his law office, then had to walk a couple of miles through heavy snow when his car couldn't make it. As soon as he heard from Vicki's mother what had happened, he hurried up to Vicki's room.

He sat on the edge of her bed — the glow from the hall light silhouetting the line of his dark hair and high cheekbones.

"Mom just told me about you and Pat." He tenderly patted her bandaged hands. "You're wonderful, honey. I'm proud of you." He leaned forward and kissed her cheek.

"I've never heard of anything like it. That black horse couldn't have impressed me more if he'd won a blue ribbon at Madison Square Garden. Standing out there like that — waiting for you to cut him free." He shook his head, scratching the back of his neck. "Beats me! The most remarkable thing was the confidence he had in you. Somehow he knew you would help him if he waited. And you didn't let him down!"

Dan Jordan rose to his feet and his fingers gently ruffled Vicki's hair.

"Come spring we'll have to do something about that pony you've been saving for. A girl like you should have a pony of her own. Good night, dear."

"Good night, Dad. See you in the morning."

Vicki lay in the dark thinking about what her dad had just said. It would be wonderful to have a pony of her own, she told herself. But, as always, her thoughts drifted toward the black horse.

At the Jockey Club, where all racing Thoroughbreds

are registered, his official name was Giant Pat. His sire was listed as Giant Killer, and his dam as One Pat. But, since he had come to Random Farm almost three years before, he was called just plain Pat. Before then he had run in numerous races — from Belmont Park to Caliente, Mexico — but when Vicki's father bought him he was sick and used up, even though he had barely reached maturity. After the age of two, and before Random Farm, his career had been a confusion of starting gates, screaming crowds, and endless shuffling between tracks in horse vans and boxcars — even an airplane, occasionally. And never in all that time had he known a home where he could stay around long enough to get acquainted.

All this Vicki learned when she had visited the Jockey Club in New York with her dad. Poor Pat. She wondered if anywhere along the way he had met anyone who loved him as dearly as she did. It was difficult for Vicki to imagine how life would be without him, now that he filled such a great part of it.

Well, at last his wandering days were over. Here with the Jordans his way of living had taken a new turn. Here there were chickens and ducks he could spar with when they invaded his pasture, and rabbits he could sniff in their hutch behind the barn. He liked Teddy, the goat, who was so bold and unafraid, and Rocky, the Irish setter — continuously cowed by the geese who came at him with necks stretched out low and mouths open, hissing like serpents. But Rosalie, always stalking and cavorting about in her own cat world, was too aloof and independent to be more than a nodding acquaintance.

Pat seemed to have a great affection for the Jordans — most of all for Vicki who adored him. But Pat had never really had a buddy of his own, a stablemate who could speak his language. There was an empty stall next to his, and many times he would stand for hours with his nose pressed against the bars that separated them. He seemed to be a happy and contented horse, but perhaps at these times he dreamed of a companion with a mane and tail and an answering whinny. Vicki liked to think that if she ever saved up enough to buy a pony, Pat would enjoy him too.

As she drifted off to sleep, she could hear the branches of the old mulberry tree scraping against the side of the house under her window. The storm had not let up. Down in the barnyard the ducks finally went indoors. And in his stall Pat peacefully munched on hay.

2. Opportunity Knocks

Every Saturday afternoon, Vicki and Kathy worked in the tackroom of the Maple Vista stable, for which they each received two dollars and fifty cents.

Most of the boarders rode their horses in the morning; and when the girls arrived after lunch, the small room would be piled with dirty, sweaty bridles and saddles.

First, the girls scrubbed them with soap and warm water and allowed them to dry. Then, they'd saddle soap them until the leather glowed with new life and the air was permeated with the fresh rich smell of it.

The smell of the leather reminded her of the time, two summers ago, when Vicki had accompanied her dad to the Miller Harness Company in New York City. He had bought a new Italian jumping saddle there. That store smelled of leather too. Vicki had pressed her face against the saddles on the racks, inhaling them, tasting them. The room glittered with all the shiny buckles and bits hanging about, and colorful horse blankets, and rows of riding coats and breeches and sparkling boots. As in a beautiful fairy tale she had walked about, caressing everything she could reach and saying to herself, "I'll take this halter for Pat and these boots for me — the ones with the black patent-leather tops, and that stunning red sheet for Pat — how well it will look on him. And some day I'll have my own saddle too, with my name engraved on a brass plate on the back of the cantle."

"How much money have you saved so far?" Kathy asked.

Vicki came out of her daydream and frowned at a particularly muddy spot on the skirt of a saddle. "Almost a hundred dollars," she answered. "Any day now I'll have enough to buy a pony."

"I'm going to buy a suit for Easter," Kathy volunteered. "I saw the neatest one in the *Times*. Mother said she'd take me shopping next week."

She held the sponge over her blonde head as if it were a hat. Then she rolled her blue eyes toward the ceiling, swayed across the floor like a fashion model, and about-faced with one hand gracefully poised under her chin.

"How do I look, Vic?"

"Like you'd better get back to work!" Mr. Broad grumbled as he came through the doorway from the stable area with another armful of tack.

Kathy rushed back to the saddle rack.

"You girls will be here until midnight if you don't get a move on."

He left the room. They remained silent until his growls died in the distance.

"It serves you right," Vicki giggled. "One of these days Mrs. Broad will walk in and then we'll both be fired. And I can't afford to — not until I get that pony!"

"Pony boy, pony boy, won't you be my pony boy," Kathy hummed.

Vicki snorted. She glared fiercely into her friend's twinkling eyes, then suddenly both were laughing uproariously and scrubbing away like a couple of fiends.

Vicki and Kathy had been inseparable since they had first met way back in kindergarten, ages ago, and their friendship had grown right along with them.

The girls had been horse crazy from the very beginning. Three years ago, when they first came to work at Maple Vista, the Broads had paid them in riding lessons instead of cash. Mrs. Broad, a competent equestrienne and instructor, gave the girls a wonderful foundation in jumping and the finer points of horsemanship. They talked of nothing but horses then. Now, Vicki noticed, Kathy was "slipping." She seemed to care less and less for horses and more and more for boys.

Yesterday, during lunch at school, Vicki told Kathy about the Watkins' mare she had been riding, how wonderful and sweet she was.

"Oh, Vicki," Kathy retorted in a voice that at times seemed painfully sophisticated. "Won't you ever grow up? Why, you're thirteen years old! Before long we'll be in college — or even married."

College! Married! Vicki clamped her teeth together and stared straight ahead. She hated it when Kathy talked like this. She hated the thought of growing up and having grown-up responsibilities.

Her dad had once explained, "Remember, honey, when you were in fourth grade how afraid you were to go into fifth grade? You thought you couldn't do the work, but when you got there it wasn't half bad. That's the way life is. As you grow up, you become more capable and more sure of yourself. When you meet new obstacles along the way you are ready for them and take them right in stride — like jumping a good hunter over an outside course. Believe me, dear, it's not as difficult as it seems. Just don't fight it and don't worry about things that haven't happened yet."

But Vicki wasn't really convinced. Even her brother Wayne was growing up. There was a time when they had spent many hours together, riding and talking about these wonderful four-legged creatures. But not any more. Well, if growing up meant giving up horses, Vicki wanted no part of it. But then again, her mom and dad loved horses and they were grown up. And what about the other adults who hunted and showed horses all the time?

She worked automatically, concentrating on the present, trying to block out the uncertain future.

By five o'clock, all the tack was clean and hanging in the proper place, ready for tomorrow. After they were paid, the girls sat silently on the grass at the edge of the Maple Vista gravel driveway, waiting for Wayne to pick

them up. Ten minutes later the Jordan station wagon crunched to a halt in front of them.

"Climb in you adorable gargoyles!" Wayne shouted. He gunned the gas pedal impatiently.

Kathy blushed as she slid into the seat beside him. Vicki knew she liked Wayne much more than she would admit.

"How come you don't ride any more?" Vicki asked her brother innocently as she hopped in and slammed the door shut.

"Other interests, little girl — more important interests, like ah —— ." He grinned handsomely, winked at Kathy.

"Girls!" Vicki supplied flatly. Her eyes were glued to the dashboard.

"And what's wrong with girls, Vick? You're one, you know!"

Vicki didn't answer. She looked out at the brown fields which were beginning to turn green. In the Jordan driveway she got out and hurried down to the barn. She was angry but didn't know why. Kathy followed, and together they fed the ducks and geese that clustered about them quacking and honking for their dinner. What a racket!

Feeding time at Random Farm was a tumultuous affair. Every creature who could give tongue was doing so. The peace and quiet of the country was only in story books. Cackling hens, squawking ducks, honking geese, baaing goat, whinnying horse, and a meowing cat; and from across the road on Watkins' Farm sheep sounds and cow sounds were all mixed together in such a hullabaloo, you'd think the creatures were being tortured, not fed.

Rocky sat silently a few yards off, watching with interest but keeping well out of reach of the hissing geese. And the rabbits were quiet, peering through the wire enclosure of their hutch, wrinkling their noses in anticipation.

When the chores were done, Kathy walked home and Vicki went back to Pat's stall for their evening talk. She called it their "talk," but actually it was just time alone together at day's end.

When all the stock had been fed, she loved to stand in Pat's stall and listen to the steady crunch of grain as he ate his evening meal. All was still about them. The barnyard noises had subsided and a wonderful afterglow of peace engulfed everything. The last rays of the setting sun lanced across the interior of the barn and gleamed on the satiny black coat of the feeding horse.

Often, Vicki would stand close to Pat with her face against his side, listening to the thump-thump of his heart — or snuggle up against him as he lay resting like a big dog. "I love you, I love you," she would whisper in his ear.

Tonight she just stood quietly admiring the "black prince." Before leaving she pressed her lips gently against his cheek. "Good night, Pat," she said under her breath, then turned and softly latched the door behind her. She felt much better now.

Vicki entered the house through the kitchen. Her mother was sitting on a stool preparing vegetables at the counter. Any time Vicki saw her, in blue jeans or riding clothes or all dressed up to go out, she had the same clean-cut look. "It's great to look like that all the time, but it's hardly worth the trouble," Vicki thought.

"When do we have dinner?" she asked and slid into a chair at the kitchen table.

"In about an hour," Mrs. Jordan answered. Without looking up she added, "Please dear, don't tilt the chair back against the radiator. It chips the paint off."

Vicki righted the chair and fished the *Patent Trader* out of the newspaper rack. Her fingers automatically found the classified section and the "Whip and Spur" column. "The same old stuff," she mumbled to herself. " 'Pony, 13.2 hands, good manners, wonderful jumper, $450. — Roan, 15 hands, spirited, 5 years old, $800.' " It read that way right down the line. Everything that sounded any good had a forbidding price tag. Out of reach — way out of reach.

"Hey, what's this?" Vicki sat bolt upright — contemplating a small ad at the bottom of the long column. "Mom," she cried out, "listen to this. 'Sturdy black and white pony, 9 years old, good temperament, saddle and bridle, $125. CArmel 6-3876.' "

"Sounds too good — must have a catch somewhere." Wayne came strolling into the kitchen. He read the ad over Vicki's shoulder. "It can't be much good for that price — especially including saddle and bridle." He whistled softly, then turned and lifted the lid off the pot roast simmering on the stove.

"M-m, does that smell good!"

"Mom, what do you think?" Vicki rose and walked over to her mother.

Bette Jordan agreed with Wayne, but she didn't say so. She read the ad slowly. "Carmel isn't too far away. Maybe Dad could take you there tomorrow. There's no harm in looking."

3. Stablemate for Pat

Every pony Vicki had ever seen was fat. Every pony she ever knew was well fed, spirited, with arched neck and round sides and rump to match. So she was hardly prepared for this little four-legged scarecrow that moved like a crab. His muzzle was completely absorbed in the sparse scattering of weeds, and the shaggy head did not lift as Vicky approached.

Close up he looked even worse. The dark forelock resembled the bunch grass that grew in the lower swamp back at Random Farm, and it was so thick she could not see the pony's eyes hidden beneath it. The mane was ragged, and dragged along the ground. Vicki bent over and lifted it to reveal the shrunken neck and bony shoulder. She let her hand wander aimlessly over the scrawny hide stretched tight around the emaciated body. Then she crouched down to examine the hairy legs and long cracked hoofs that badly needed trimming. There was an ache in her throat as her eyes took in the flanks that sucked inward and the hipbones that pushed outward, threatening to break through the skin. She stepped back and walked behind the pony, noticed the tent-shaped rump and the concave sides and the tail — long, greasy, knotted with burrs.

Vicki drew in a painful deep breath and looked up at her dad. Neither one spoke. The pony continued to gnaw his way along the beaten earth — ignoring the girl and her father and the short fat man who owned him. The bright spring sun was directly overhead and the warm air hummed with the steady drone of insects.

The fat man cleared his throat. "Got no use for him, now that the kids have gotten too big for him — but he's a good pony, and tough."

Vicki thought, "I'll bet he's tough. He would have been dead a long time ago if he weren't." But she didn't speak.

"I don't think he'll suit." Her dad's voice, aimed at the fat man, cut through her thoughts.

"He's too small, too run down. It would take months to build him up — get him to look like a pony again." Then to Vicki, he said, "Come on honey, let's go."

Vicki followed her dad across the lot to the station wagon parked beside the fat man's house. Her mind was whirling around and around, vainly seeking one good reason to buy this unfortunate creature. As she trod slowly past the back porch her mouth watered, for the air here was filled with the tantalizing smell of frying bacon and eggs. She was hungry. Then suddenly she looked back at the half-starved pony grubbing to stay alive. The hunger pang stuck in her middle.

"Dad!" She caught her father's sleeve. "Dad, let me buy him — please let me buy him!"

Her father stopped as if he had come up against a stone wall. He turned slowly to face his daughter, and Vicki's voice cracked as it leaped ahead, gaining momentum.

"Look at him, Dad! He's skin and bones. If I don't buy him, he'll never make it!"

Her father opened his mouth to speak but Vicki couldn't stop now.

"I can take him home and turn him out in the pasture and watch him grow round and fat. He won't cost much to feed in the winter. I can earn —— "

"But Vicki," her dad interrupted gently, "you've been saving your money for over two years to buy a pony. This one is too small for you to ride — much too small. I know how you feel. It hurts to think what lies ahead for him, but you can't take in every friendless starved animal in the country. The world is filled with this sort of thing — everywhere you look."

The fat man went on into the house. The screen door slammed shut behind him and from somewhere within a woman's voice screeched and a baby began to cry. Vicki felt like crying too. Her father stared toward the closed door, then back at the pony and down at Vicki again. At this moment he could understand his daughter's agony and despair.

Vicki had gained control of her voice, "I *know* I can't rescue every friendless animal in the world," she stammered, "but here is one I can. Dad, I *want* to buy this pony!"

Vicki paid one hundred dollars for the pony — minus saddle and bridle. She and her dad came for him that same afternoon in a pickup Mr. Jordan had borrowed from his neighbor. The truck was backed against an embankment and an old stall door was laid against the rear end to form a ramp. The pony came aboard as if his head was too heavy to carry. Now he was wearing a soft leather halter in place of the wide hard collar which had worn away the hair behind his ears. He was cross-tied behind the cab. All the way home the forlorn little pony stood quietly, his furry head almost touching the floor and his short legs braced against the lurching vehicle.

All the way home Vicki kept looking back to see how her pony was doing. She felt wonderful. She hadn't decided on a name for him yet, but that could wait. Now she was anxious to get home, to have him meet her mom, and Rocky, and Rosalie the cat, and the ducks and rabbits, and chickens, and Teddy the goat. Above all she wondered how Pat would feel about having this miserable-looking creature as his stablemate.

4. The Worming

Vicki never got around to naming the pony herself. But the kids on Dingle Ridge did after word got around that the little "rascal" had bitten Toby Carpenter, the pesty boy from Eight Bells Farm. Nobody saw the pony bite him but Toby said he did — "for no reason at all."

"That's what *he* says," thought Vicki. That pesty Toby was always doing something bad — kicking at the chickens as they came out of the hen house, or teasing Teddy the goat when he was tethered and couldn't fight back. And once, Vicki found two chickens locked in the feed bin. If she hadn't come along and freed them, they might have suffocated. She could never prove who did it, but the type of crime pointed directly to Toby who "never did nothing."

After Toby had spread the news of the biting incident, the small fry on Dingle Ridge called the pony Jesse James the Outlaw. They said he looked like an outlaw too, with his long forelock falling down over his right eye. The left one, cold and blue, had a nasty look which completed the sinister picture of the lawbreaker. The name stuck, but in a little while it was shortened to just plain Jesse.

This was the day Jesse was to be wormed. He had been locked in the big box stall next to Pat's since yesterday afternoon. He hadn't had a lick of food in all that time and wouldn't get any until three hours after the worming. Wayne told Vicki the worm medicine worked best on an empty stomach, and Wayne knew all about these things.

Vicki straddled the uppermost fork of the tall maple and peered anxiously up Dingle Ridge Road. It was almost ten o'clock now and getting hotter every minute. She had been waiting here almost two hours, watching the road below and hoping Dr. Regan would arrive before poor Jesse starved to death.

When she saw his old Chevy rumble into view around the hairpin turn she scrambled down from her perch and met the doctor as he climbed out of his car in front of the barn.

Vicki liked Dr. Regan. She liked his soft drawl and big gentle hands, but most of all she adored his smell, which was all mixed up with iodine and disinfectant and horses.

"How's my girl today?" The doctor spoke past the pipe clamped between his teeth.

"Fine, thank you." Vicki smiled uncertainly, then straddled the white board fence alongside the automobile and thoughtfully watched the doctor. His glasses flashed and his bald head gleamed in the sunlight as he bent forward to slip into a pair of white coveralls. He reached into the back seat for his black leather bag, and, as he knocked his pipe against the fence post and turned toward the barn door, Vicki slid to the ground and ran to the house for Wayne.

She always called Wayne when a crisis was pending. He was her hero even though she would never tell him that. He had a hero look — tall and slender with sandy hair and blue eyes that looked straight at you when he talked. Kathy said he was cute — Vicki thought handsome was a better word, especially when he wore the blue and gold football uniform of Granville High. Now she pried him loose from the sports section of the Sunday *Times* and together they headed back down to the barn.

Jesse was already cross-tied when they got there. Pat's head was over his stall door. He seemed only mildly interested. This was old stuff to him; he went through it twice a year. But the pony didn't know what was about to happen, and at this point didn't seem to care much.

He had been here for almost a week now. After the Toby Carpenter incident, none of the kids in the neighborhood would have anything to do with him — but that didn't bother him because all he cared about right now was eating. Just about anything would do as long as it grew up from the ground or hung down from a tree. He drank water too — as though he couldn't get enough.

On the day of his arrival he drank seven ten-quart pails of water and just about the same amount every day thereafter. Vicki was afraid he would burst. An ordinary horse might, but Jesse was not an ordinary horse. He was a Shetland pony — small, rugged, compact. His ancestors had worked in the coal mines — many of them without ever seeing the light of day. They were miniature draft horses, built to survive under the worst conditions, and Jesse was no exception.

Now he stood braced, hungry as a bear but defiant. His fur-filled ears twitched and his nostrils quivered suspiciously, but through the heavy forelock that splashed halfway down his face his eyes were steady and unafraid as he watched Vicki and Wayne, and Dr. Regan with the cold shiny syringe jutting out of his hand.

Four days before, Mr. Shannon the blacksmith had trimmed the pony's hoofs, cutting away long ragged cartilage that had probably been growing and spreading since the pony was born.

And later that week, Vicki in a bathing suit and armed with a huge brush and plenty of soap, had shown Jesse that water was used for things other than drinking. She tied him up short on a fence post and there beneath the warm afternoon sun gave him the washing of his life. The snowy lather bubbled and foamed over both of them as she scrubbed him down from the soft pink nose to the farthest tip of his tail. She rinsed him with a hose, and scrubbed and rinsed again — three times until the large black markings shone bright and clear against his skinny white body.

She sympathized with the sad-faced pony throughout the entire operation. She knew how he felt — a bath was an awful nuisance. But nevertheless, when she was done, she stepped back and surveyed him with deep satisfac-

tion. Ten pounds of dirt must have come off. The pony
looked even thinner than he had when she first saw him,
but at least he was clean and you didn't have to hold your
nose when you came near him.

Another day, he was cross-tied again. This time he had
his mane pulled. Wayne was good at pulling a mane.
Vicki had watched him do Pat's many times. He would

grasp the hair in little tufts, perhaps a dozen hairs at a time, always choosing the longest, then pull them out by the roots. He continued to work up and down the mane until it was all the same length and thinness. Pat's mane was easy to do because he stood as steady as a rock. Vicki was always afraid of hurting him, but Wayne assured her that the nerves on a horse's neck were very insensitive to pain. But Jesse was so much smaller than Pat that with each downard pull Wayne nearly knocked the little fellow off his feet. Vicki objected much more than Jesse did.

"Why can't we just trim it with scissors?" she asked.

"Because then it would stick up straight like a porcupine."

"Why should it? The barber cuts your hair with scissors and it doesn't stick up."

"That's different," Wayne countered between plucks. "My hair doesn't need thinning to stay down, but Jesse's does."

Finally it was over. The mane lay neat and flat against his neck and Jesse stood knee-deep in pony hair — enough to fill a couple of pillows.

He was shifted back to the small enclosed pasture behind the barn and just when he began to feel that things were looking up again Vicki had shoved him into the stall next to Pat's and left him there to starve the day before the worming.

Now, as something else was about to be done to him, he didn't make any commotion — just stood quietly, waiting. But as the nozzle of the wicked-looking syringe came closer, his ears flattened and his nostrils dilated.

"Better put a hand on him, Wayne." The doctor's voice was casual. He had been doctoring horses for over thirty years and knew enough not to take any situation for granted — which went double for ponies. Horses might be bigger and more powerful, but ponies were craftier and more resourceful.

Vicki hung back. She wanted no part of this. She wished she could leave, but something held her glued in place.

Wayne unhooked the cross-tie chains, then snapped a lead shank to Jesse's halter. He cradled the pony's head in his arms, forcing the muzzle upward so that Dr. Regan could slide the syringe into his mouth.

Wayne was very strong and quite sure of himself around horses. Before this moment Vicki had never seen the horse that Wayne couldn't handle. But today in about two seconds, one small pony shattered his record.

Jesse had had it. He had tolerated the hoof clippers and the bath and the mane-pulling without a whimper. But someone trying to shoot a pint of white slimy goo down his throat was too much. With one loud belching cough he spewed the white liquid back into Dr. Regan's face. It seemed as if more came out than went in, for suddenly the window and walls and floor were spattered with the stuff. He reared back, then with one violent shake sent Wayne flying through the door like a rag doll. Wayne stumbled over the mounting block; then, swinging his arms madly in a frantic effort to regain his balance, fell

headfirst into the manure pile. Jesse went through the doorway just two jumps behind Wayne. Vicki made a desperate grab for the halter rope that trailed behind him — but missed.

Up the slope went the pony, bucking and tossing his head, trying to get rid of the awful taste on his tongue. He rounded the corner of the barn and made a beeline for the sheep-covered meadow across Dingle Ridge. Chickens shrieked and ducks squawked as the enraged pony charged through them. He scooted across the barnyard, and so intent was his mad flight that he never noticed the taut rope almost six inches above the ground. One end of it was attached to Teddy the goat, the other end to an iron stake. Teddy staggered to his knees and the stake ripped loose from the earth as the pony slammed against the rope. Jesse skidded across the grass on his chin, flipped over once, then bounced back to his feet and was off again, barely missing his stride. The metal snap on the end of his trailing halter shank snagged in the rolling metal stake, whipping it along behind.

Teddy was now in the race too. He and Jesse were running neck and neck with a thirty-foot length of rope zinging along between them. The end came quickly. They passed Vicki's maple tree at full gallop, Teddy to the left and Jesse to the right, then abruptly found themselves whirling around the huge trunk in opposite directions.

By the time Vicki arrived they were hopelessly wrapped around the tree. Wayne came slowly up from the barn, shaking and brushing the manure out of his

hair. Dr. Regan was close behind mopping himself with a towel. They were both as mad as a couple of hornets. Vicki tried to keep a straight face but a giggle broke through — then another and another.

Wayne said, "I don't think it's so funny."

Then he too began to chuckle. Dr. Regan tuned in next and by the time Mom and Dad came down from the house to see what all the commotion was about, they were all roaring with laughter.

Only Teddy and Jesse didn't see the humor in it.

It took almost fifteen minutes to get them free of each other. When he was back at the barn the pony took his medicine quietly. He was too exhausted to resist.

As he pulled out of the driveway, Dr. Regan called, "We'll try to give him another worming next Saturday — works better that way."

Vicki moaned and Wayne laughed as he put his arm around her shoulder.

"OK, Doc," he shouted. "We'll be waiting for you!"

5. Troublemaker

The coming of Jesse to Random Farm revealed a side of Pat's Thoroughbred nature the Jordans had never suspected. Pat promptly became the pony's big brother and protector.

But Jesse didn't need any protection. He could take care of himself. He had his own ideas of how things should be done, and the fact that Pat was bigger than he — didn't faze him one bit. He'd been around a long time, longer than Pat, and he was a pony, therefore smarter and craftier to begin with. To put it simply, he knew the ropes, and as soon as he recovered from his malnutrition, which took all of one month, Jesse set about converting the black horse to the ways of the wicked.

First — Jesse was an escape artist. He could open any latch on the place, he could unfasten any hook — even untie a knot when necessary. It was no wonder his former owner had buckled a heavy leather collar around his neck and tied him securely to a steel stake.

There were continuous complaints from neighbors.

"Come get your pony out of here, he's in my garden!"
"Your pony is trimming our hedges — badly!" "He's gotten into our corn patch!" "Rolling in the asparagus bed."
"Eating my tulips." "Chasing our cows." An endless flow
of protests, until the Jordans began feeling they had taken
on one more animal than they could handle.

Bette Jordan caught the brunt of it. Vicki and Wayne
were in school and her husband, Dan, was in the city. Too
often she'd come in from shopping to the tune of the
clanging phone, then drop everything to go chase the
Shetland over the countryside. When she cornered him
and snapped a shank to his halter, he would come along
quietly — sometimes. Other times, she would ride him
out — go bucking off down the road toward home. She
was a good rider and this was no problem, but the day he
messed up a neighbor's flower beds was the last straw.

From the school bus window, Vicki saw a black and
white pony galloping down Finch Road.

"That's Jesse!" she cried.

"Oh, Buzz," she called to the driver. "Can you let me
off here — I just saw my pony running loose. I'd better
catch him before he gets into trouble."

Buzz pulled up on the shoulder of Dingle Ridge. Kathy
had been absent that day and Wayne was stretched out on
the back seat eating an apple.

"Will you take my books, Wayne?" she asked. "I've got
to chase down that pony. Just saw him through the window."

Her brother sat up. "Can you manage it alone?" His

words were mixed up with crunching apple.

"Sure, I can handle him," she yelled back as she hopped down the steps and charged off in the direction Jesse had taken.

The Shetland had stopped running and was standing at the entrance of a neighbor's driveway, munching on a daisy patch. One look at him convinced her he had no intention of being caught.

Mrs. Jordan came panting along. She was wearing her favorite white blouse and blue flannel slacks, and even though she was angry and out of breath, her flushed face was lovely and her short, light-brown hair unruffled.

"This will probably take two of us," she said. As if on signal, Jesse wheeled and jogged up the driveway, stopping occasionally for a quick nibble but always keeping a wary eye on his pursuers. He circled the large rambling white house at a walk, keeping just out of reach and plowing up the immaculate flower beds as he went his merry, unhurried way.

There seemed to be no one at home. This was small consolation, for the damage he was doing would have to be paid for anyway.

The second time around, Vicki whispered. "You keep after him, Mom, I'll wait right here at this corner."

She flattened her body against the wall like the heroine in some cloak-and-dagger movie. In a moment she heard the bushes crackle and the tramp of little hoofs.

"Here he comes — Now!"

She leaped to meet the pony as he came around the

corner. He slammed on his brakes and pivoted sharply away, but Vicki had already latched on to his halter.

"We got him!" she screeched victoriously as the pony halted. This was the way he usually reacted to being caught. The moment anyone put a hand on his halter, he gave up.

Her mother walked up behind the pony. "I'll ride him home, Vick. My shoes are pretty muddy now, but the rest of me will be too if I keep sloshing around through this mess." The road was muddy and pock-marked with brown pools of water left by the morning's rain. Mrs. Jordan snapped one end of the shank she was carrying to the pony's halter and quickly fashioned an emergency rein. With one quick step and jump, she straddled the pony's

back. Vicki caught hold of the end of his tail and slogged along behind. "This is great," she commented. "It makes walking so easy."

Suddenly Jesse began running toward home. "Whoa, whoa!" Vicki yelled, sliding and hanging back, plowing along through the mud like an outboard motorboat.

"Whoa, Jesse!" she cried again and jerked back on his tail with all her might.

Then, Jesse did it, as only Jesse could. He dropped his head, bucked once and shied violently to the left. Bette Jordan was thrown off his back and flew through the air as if she had been shot out of a cannon. At the same instant, the pony swung his quarters to the right and the whiplash of his tail sent Vicki flying. Mother and daughter converged on a large muddy pool as if the pony had aimed them at it. And Jesse, without so much as a backward glance, tossed his head defiantly as he bounded on ahead.

Vicki sat up in the muck, staring at her mother in speechless horror. She scrambled to her feet and helped Mrs. Jordan to hers.

"Oh wow, Mother!" she sputtered. "I'm awfully sorry. I shouldn't have pulled his tail so hard."

Bette Jordan was too angry to speak. As she wiped the mud from her face she glared after the fast-departing pony. Even though she was covered from head to foot in mud, her poise was remarkable. She shook her head slowly from side to side and suddenly began to laugh. Then she stopped and looked at her daughter.

"Vicki," she said in mock seriousness. "Your face is dirty."

After that episode, all spare time was spent patching fences and converting gates. Where a single rail around the pasture would hold Pat, they found Jesse could duck under — so a second rail had to be added. Then a third when they found places where Jesse could crawl under.

To add insult to injury, Jesse decided it was time to take Pat along on those escapades. When he became aware that the black horse could not squeeze through the tight places he could, Jesse had to think of another way out.

The first indication of this came in the form of a phone call from the Johnsons who lived about a mile down the road — "A pony and a black horse are grazing in our back yard."

"How the devil did they get out this time?" Dad asked.

Another inspection was made. Bette, Dan, Vicki, and Wayne examined all the fences minutely. They couldn't find one opening big enough for a pony to go through, certainly not a thousand-pound horse.

They set up a watch system, but crafty little Jesse seemed to know what was going on. He wouldn't make one false move if he suspected someone was watching. As soon as their backs were turned, though, both Jesse and Pat were gone again.

The pasture was surrounded on three sides by post-and-rail fence. The fourth side — the west side — was bounded by heavy timber which sloped off sharply through jagged rock and underbrush, so thick and treacherous a mountain goat would think twice before entering it. This was the only possible avenue of escape left and, though it seemed a highly improbable one, Vicki and her dad decided to look into it.

Vicki was the first to discover a hoofprint in this impenetrable jungle. Then she and Dan Jordan discovered another and another. They tracked along, ripping their clothes on brambles, climbing over fallen trees, and squeezing between rugged outcrops. One hour later they came out on Dingle Ridge, about a mile from home, and found the runaways.

In three years Pat had never left his pasture, then along

came one little fur-covered scamp — and now the Jordans had *two* "vagabonds" to contend with.

A new post-and-rail fence was built. The Jordans constructed it on a weekend, and when the job was done, the pasture fencing was tight enough to hold a chipmunk.

The horse and pony gave up then. It probably didn't really matter anyway — they had each other. They were inseparable. Vicki enjoyed watching them cavort around the pasture. They would follow each other at a gallop, first one in the lead, then the other. Suddenly they would wheel and kick out, then swap ends and spar for an opening like two boxers, except that in their game anything was fair — hoof or teeth or a combination of both. Vicki was always afraid one of them would get hurt — especially Pat. But it was all in fun.

6. A Dangerous Predicament

Summer rolled on into late August. The nights were cooling down. The mornings found the leaves tipped with color, and along the stone walls the poison ivy was already turning red. Soon autumn would be here and along with it the official opening of the fox-hunting season. Dan Jordan rode Pat almost every day. He wanted to be in fit condition for hunting, and for the Golden's Bridge Hounds horse show which would take place this year on the Von Gal estate on the first Saturday in September.

The night before the show, Vicki, Kathy, Wayne, and Dan Jordan were busy in the barn, cleaning tack and preparing the horses for the morning. The Watkins had loaned their two, Loli and Jeanie, to help round out the Jordan hunt team which would compete against eight other teams in the last event of the day.

The Watkins were the best neighbors anyone could ever have. Their farm lay directly across the road from the Jordan place, but it was much larger, over two hundred acres of lovely rolling fields and woodland.

They had sheep and black Angus cattle and chickens and turkeys and some fancy white Japanese geese — and such an assortment of dogs — labradors, dachshunds, basset hounds, golden retrievers — that Vicki couldn't figure out how they kept all their names straight.

Both Mr. and Mrs. Watkins were very generous. Mr. Watkins had suggested that the Jordans use their horses and trailer, since he and his wife and ten-year-old daughter, Lisa, would be in Maine for the weekend.

So, as things stood now, Dan Jordan would show Pat in the hunter division, and Vicki and Kathy would see what they could do on Loli and Jeanie. Wayne would drive the Jeep and trailer hitch, and be their groom — a job he reluctantly accepted after much coaxing.

Mrs. Jordan was on the trophy committee, and earlier that evening the girls had helped her polish the silver trophies which would be awarded.

"Wouldn't you just love to win this one!" Vicki exclaimed, holding aloft a sparkling silver cup.

"It won't be so easy," commented her mother. "Most of the classes have fifteen or twenty entries, made up of some of the best riders and horses from Fairfield and Ox Ridge — plus some top-rate upstaters."

She paused and smiled. "Remember, girls, there are only four ribbons awarded to a class and just the blue gets a trophy. So don't get your hopes too high."

"It doesn't matter anyway," chirped Kathy. "It's the game that counts, not who wins."

Vicki nodded in agreement but when she was competing, she had a dauntless drive to win. Now, standing atop an upturned box, she painstakingly braided Pat's mane.

She wished she could be riding him instead of Loli tomorrow. But her dad permitted no one else to ride Pat — not even his daughter. He was a horseman who believed that every equestrian rode differently. And a horse, because he was a creature of habit who learned by repetition, could perform better under the steady, consistent training of one rider. This was the rule and Vicki obeyed it. She had long ago resigned herself to the fact that she must not ride the black horse. But nothing could keep her from loving him.

At the other end of the barn, Kathy was studiously working over Jeanie. And in a stall, Wayne's nimble fingers were quickly fashioning a row of short neat braids along the crest of Loli's neck. Dan Jordan walked about, supervising operations, and Jesse, whose head barely reached the top of his stall door, watched as best he could.

The scene was at once peaceful and expectant. The air was warm with the aroma of horses, hay, and polished leather.

When their tails were braided and taped up for the night, the horses had light sheets strapped around them to keep them clean till morning.

Kathy stayed at the Jordans' overnight. The show grounds were almost eight miles away and the first class started at nine o'clock sharp. Though both girls were dead tired, they were too restless to sleep and spent over two

hours rearranging Vicki's room. Just before they flopped into bed, exhausted, Vicki pushed back the white ruffled curtains, so that the morning sun would waken them if the alarm clock failed.

They slept fitfully and were up at the first crack of dawn — polishing boots.

Then Vicki rummaged through her dresser drawers till she found her old faded yellow shirt.

"Are you going to wear that old thing?" Kathy exclaimed, as Vicki set up her ironing board and plugged in the iron.

"I sure am — it's my good-luck shirt — wouldn't ride in a horse show without it."

"Oh, that's silly. An old yellow shirt can't make you win."

"Maybe not," rejoined Vicki, "but it protects me — it really does."

Kathy arched her eyebrows. "Come on, Vick. Weren't you wearing that shirt the day you broke your collarbone? Didn't bring you much luck that time, did it?"

"Oh, yes, it did! Think how badly I could have been hurt, if I hadn't had this shirt on."

Kathy gave up in disgust.

From the kitchen, Mrs. Jordan called, "Breakfast is ready."

Dad and Wayne were already eating their pancakes when the girls came down. Fresh batter sizzled on the hot pan. The sun was streaming through the window. What a gorgeous day it was going to be!

Since the trailer hitch could only accommodate two horses, Mr. Broad had agreed to transport the third. He arrived at eight with his horse van. Pat was quickly led aboard and tied securely in a narrow straight stall. There were five other occupants in the vehicle waiting impatiently to be on their way.

As the van wheeled out of the driveway, Mr. Broad yelled back, "See you at the show grounds."

Wayne taxied the Watkins' Jeep and trailer hitch into the barnyard. "All aboard, that's going aboard," he sang cheerfully from the driver's seat.

The girls were ready and waiting with Loli and Jeanie. The horses had felt wraps around their legs and leather helmets on their heads to protect them from the swing and sway of the journey. They loaded quietly with no fuss. The tail gate was lifted into position and bolted.

Wayne tapped the horn softly, "Hurry, hurry, hurry! Mother and Dad have already gone on!"

Vicki and Kathy jumped in and the three crammed together in the front seat. The Jeep crept out of the drive and around the hairpin turn to the tune of Jesse's anxious cries from the barn. They began the long steep pull to Route 121.

As they neared the top of the grade, Vicki sighed. "On our way at last," she said.

A backward jolt threw them forward, then snapped them back. They sat bolt upright for a second, immobilized by the sudden shock.

"What's wrong?" Vicki gasped. "What happened?"

Wayne's foot was jammed down on the brake, but the Jeep was slipping slowly backward.

"Quick, Vick," he yelled. "Take a look back there, I think the trailer's come loose."

Vicki practically fell out of the Jeep in her eagerness to obey. She slid on the gravel as she rushed around to the rear, then stopped dead in her tracks when she saw what had happened.

The trailer connection had been jerked out of the socket that held it fast to the Jeep. Only a thin safety chain kept them together now. The slightest tug would sever the link and send the trailer plummeting downhill into certain disaster.

"Holy cow, Vick, what are you staring at back there? I can't hold this thing here forever."

Wayne had the door open, leaning as far out as he could, trying to see what was happening. One of the horses, probably Jeanie, began kicking the side of the trailer. Vicki dashed around behind. Over the top of the tail gate she could see Loli's head trying to peer around, but the cross-tie chains held her fast. Behind them the dirt road dropped away steeply and curved sharply to the left.

"Set the emergency brake," she screamed. "Let's get these horses out before the trailer breaks away!"

In a flash of memory Vicki saw the horse van that had turned over several months ago at the intersection of Routes 121 and 6. She could still hear the horses thrashing and screaming inside — trapped in the wreckage.

"I can't set the emergency," Wayne yelled back. "It won't hold!"

Kathy sat stiffly erect, glued to the seat. Vicki charged back to her brother.

"Didn't you check that hitch before we started?" Her voice was completely out of control.

"No, that was your job!" he roared back.

Panic was rapidly taking over, robbing them both of their reason — crippling their ingenuity.

"Hold it, everyone, hold it!" Suddenly Wayne was in command of himself again. Now was no time to argue about who was responsible for what.

"Kathy," he said as calmly as he could. "Get out there and give Vicki a hand. Try to get a couple of rocks against the rear tires of the trailer. Maybe we can hold it in place until I back the Jeep into position."

Kathy came out of her trance and rushed out to Vicki's assistance. Together they began dragging a huge boulder across the road, but it kept slipping out of their clutching fingers.

Jeanie was kicking in earnest now — rocking the trailer. Vicki let go of the boulder and rushed up to the tail gate. She grasped the lever that locked it and hung all her weight, trying to pry it open.

"I've got to get these horses out!"

But it held fast as if it were in a vice. The girls frantically jammed their backs against the vehicle, but their feet kept slipping and sliding in the gravel as the tremendous weight above pressed down upon them.

Wayne threw the Jeep into gear and began gunning the motor against the backward drag. The safety chain was taut now, vibrating against the increasing strain.

Suddenly, around the bend, a milk truck lumbered into view. The driver braked to a halt a half-dozen yards behind the trailer — there was no room to pass.

"Please, mister!" The words came tumbling out as Vicki rushed over to the cab. "Could you bring the nose of your truck up against this trailer? It's coming loose. We've got to hold it in place so our Jeep can back down to it."

The florid-faced driver peered out of the side window, sizing up their situation.

"Well, I don't know," he hesitated. "I don't want to be responsible for maybe denting the rear end of that trailer. You know, my insurance won't cover — "

"Mister, if you don't hold that trailer," Vicki pleaded, "in about two minutes we're going to have an awful mess around here." Tears sprang to her eyes, fogging her vision.

"All right, all right." This was more than the driver could take. He gunned the motor. "OK, girl — stand there and guide me in."

The truck inched slowly forward. Vicki's raised hand motioned him on, then signaled a halt when his bumper pressed against the tail gate. The driver set his emergency brake and got out. Wayne allowed the Jeep to come back until the trailer arm was directly above the socket. When Vicki and the driver clamped them together, Kathy quickly slipped in the safety pin.

"Thank you, oh, thank you!" Vicki grabbed the driver's hand and began shaking it. "I don't know what we would have done if you hadn't come along."

"That's all right, miss." The driver smiled and flushed as he withdrew his hand, pulled out a red kerchief, and began mopping the back of his neck.

Behind the wheel once more, he called gruffly, "Now let's get that thing out of here so I can deliver this milk before it goes sour."

They were almost at the show grounds before anyone spoke.

"Wow was that close — Lady Luck was with us that time!" The color was just beginning to return to Wayne's face.

"It must have been the yellow shirt," muttered Kathy.

7. The Horse Show

Wayne guided the Jeep into the parking area where numerous vans were already lined up. Grooms were stripping horses of their traveling wraps, repairing loose braids, wiping away road dust, applying hoof oil — like barbers putting the finishing touches on their customers. Some riders stood by waiting impatiently, others were already in the saddle, warming up.

Mr. Jordan rode over on Pat while they were unloading. Wayne quickly told about their near disaster.

"Oh, I wish you had been with us," Vicki chimed in.

Mr. Jordan chuckled. "I'm glad I wasn't — would have gone all to pieces." He placed a quieting hand on Pat's neck. The black horse was bouncing in place, anxious to move out.

"You had better mount up, girls — show's almost ready to begin."

Vicki's nerves were jumping too, but as soon as she mounted Loli she felt better, more relaxed, for she had always gotten on well with the little bay Throughbred and enjoyed riding her. Kathy swung aboard Jeanie and side by side they trotted ahead.

The white Von Gal mansion made a dazzling backdrop to the show grounds. They jogged past the ever-present red ambulance and an enormous ring where the hack and pony classes would be held. Early spectators were moving about in groups talking quietly. Up ahead was a tall, striped tent, which housed the refreshment stand and announcers' booth. The girls checked in, picked up their numbers, and hooked them to the backs of their coat collars.

Schooling over the outside course was prohibited at this late hour, but Vicki decided to circle the field and get a close-up view of the types of obstacles to be negotiated. While Kathy stopped to chat with a boy she knew from school, Vicki went on alone.

First came the brush fence, then the wooden coop, and a short way after the first turn, the log jump. She walked Loli downgrade, swung right to the white gate, then on to the in-and-out. She slowed here to study the arrangement of these two post-and-rail fences perhaps twenty-seven feet apart. She knew there was no room for error at this one. Jump the first fence, one stride, and jump the second. That was the only way to cross these obstacles correctly; and it would require a careful control of pace.

Vicki continued on to the next, another solidly built rail fence, then right and up the hill to the aiken, an eight-foot spread of brush with a rail on top which gave a horse a chance to stand back, jump big, and finish with a flourish. She liked this kind and so did Loli.

The show had a good turnout and the entries were heavy as Mrs. Jordan had predicted.

Vicki almost took a ribbon in the first class, the Hunter Hack, where all horses were judged on manners at the walk, trot, and canter. There were fourteen entries. After the first ten minutes seven were eliminated, which left Vicki in the ring with six others. Her chances looked good. Loli was smooth and responsive — at her best, then suddenly a spectator accidentally dropped his hat over the rail and Loli shied and put in two quick bucks right smack in front of the judge. And that finished that.

Their next class was over the outside course. Loli's performance wasn't too bad, but at least four others were better, including Pat who took a second place.

"Nice going, Dad!" Vicki called, then dismounted and gave Pat's neck a great big hug and kiss.

"I think we ought to pole Loli before your next class," advised Mr. Jordan. "She's rubbing her fences."

Kathy, her face beaming, came jogging over on Jeanie. A yellow third-place ribbon was streaming from the pony's browband. Wayne walked alongside carrying Jeanie's plaid-wool cooler draped over his shoulder.

"That Pony-Hack class was real stiff," he proudly announced. "It's tough to win anything in that kind of company." Then he affectionately slapped the little chestnut across the rump.

Kathy was in seventh heaven. Vicki couldn't keep the envy out of her eyes. Because she was just fourteen-hands-two-inches tall, Jeanie could enter the pony division. Any animal over that height had to compete against horses. The little mare had quality and moved out freely which gave her a decided advantage over her pony-gaited competition. Vicki knew that to win on Loli was much more difficult, but that was no reason to deny her best friend this moment of victory. "You're a bad sport," she told herself.

"Congratulations, Kathy," she called, and smiled warmly when their eyes met.

The noon break was called. The horses were unsaddled and put back into the vans where they could rest and munch hay until the afternoon session.

The Jordans had brought a picnic lunch. They spread it out under a huge maple tree close to the vans. Kathy's parents joined the party, and shared the delicious cold fried chicken and potato chips and ice-cold lemonade. Afterwards there were cookies and fresh fruit. Kathy's mother looked very trim and pretty in a white blouse and skirt. The Jordans said nothing to her of the trailer incident because she was a worrier. Though she was happy to see her daughter ride, she fretted constantly, always expecting the worst would happen. Bob Field, Kathy's father, was just the opposite — relaxed and at ease. He and Mr. Jordan smoked and discussed politics while Wayne stretched out on the grass in front of them, with his hat across his eyes, trying to nap.

The girls sat silently by themselves gazing out across the show grounds. Kathy was happy with the way things were going. Vicki brooded, frowning into the warm sun, mentally riding her horse, trying to correct the mistakes she had already made and the ones she might make this afternoon. There I go again, she thought, worrying about the things that haven't happened.

At one o'clock Mr. Jordan poled Loli in a small field behind the vans. A low post and rail had been set up there for this kind of schooling. He stood beside the fence, holding one end of a bamboo pole that was resting across the top bar.

"OK, Vicki," he called to his daughter who sat on her horse almost thirty yards away. "Bring her on."

Loli came in at a slow canter and jumped. Dan Jordan brought up the bamboo pole, striking her lightly across the front and hind legs as she went over. The mare thought she had gauged the height correctly but the rap across her legs changed her mind. The third time over, she folded her legs better and jumped a good bit higher so as to assure clearance. Vicki always felt this was a dirty trick to play on a horse, but as her dad had told her many times, "It's better for him, and better for you. If he jumps clean, it lessens the danger of hooking a fence and maybe a bad fall."

The loudspeaker blared, "Next over the outside course, Working Hunter, amateur to ride."

Vicki lined up with twelve other entries. Mr. Jordan was astride Pat, calmly waiting beside her. "How can he be so relaxed?" she thought. Her own stomach was doing flip-flops.

Five horses went before her number was called. She watched each performance like a hawk — judging every stride, every jump. "That coop was taken too close — the gate too far back. The in-and-out was offstride — awkward."

"Number 8, next over the outside course."

"That's for us," she whispered to the mare, then picked

up her reins, made one circle at a trot, then broke into a canter and was on her way.

Loli jumped the brush as if it was ten feet high and the coop the same way. She's arching too high, getting in too close, she thought. But the jumps were all clean. Vicki pulled up after her last fence feeling a whole lot better.

On a small rise of ground she leaned forward and anxiously braced herself for Pat's round. She was almost afraid to look — afraid something dreadful might happen to him. The black horse seemed to be on springs — his neck arched forward into the bit as Mr. Jordan cantered toward the first fence. She held her breath as she watched him measure his stride and smoothly clear the obstacle. When he rubbed the coop her heart dropped into her boots, then soared aloft as he flew over the log jump. She "rode" Pat all the way around the course, feeling every beat of his hoofs, rating him carefully into each fence. Her hands were sweating as he approached the last jump. Her shoulders lifted as he leaped, and slumped exhausted when he landed.

Mr. Jordan rode up beside her. Pat reached forward and began scratching his forehead against her knee. She was about to lean down to kiss his itchy face when Mr. Jordan unconsciously pulled it away. "I guess we didn't take anything for that round," he commented, then swung the black horse toward the parking field. Vicki said nothing and as she jogged along behind, the loudspeaker announced that the riders from Ox Ridge had taken first, second, third, and fourth — a clean sweep.

Vicki and her dad were resting their horses in the shade of a van when Kathy came galloping up. "Hey folks, they're organizing the hunt teams — let's go!"

The three cantered slowly toward the outside course. Most of the teams were already assembled — waiting for the start. Mr. Jordan pulled up near the in-gate and held a brief conference with the girls.

"Vicki, Loli goes better in front, so you lead off on her. Keep a good even hunting pace, not too fast and not too slow."

"I know what to do — you've told me a thousand times."

"That may be — but I'm telling you again."

He turned to Kathy. "You're second. Hold your distance, maybe fifty yards — don't crowd up on Loli." He paused to let his words sink in before he went on. "I'll be third man. I'll try to maintain the same distance as there is between you two. If you close up, I'll close, if you widen, I'll widen. In that way our team will look even and controlled all the way around."

They were all set now, ten teams ready to go — two more than had been expected.

The Meadowbrook team went first. The two girls watched them go. It was lovely to see the three riders in tandem galloping over the course. They closed up too much before the in-and-out, but they weren't bad at all. A resounding cheer rose from the spectators as they came in over the last fence.

The next team was also from Meadowbrook. But their

lead horse quit at the log jump which fouled them up completely.

Lois Evans, the leader of number three team, smiled over at Vicki as she kissed her rabbit's foot, and jammed it into her vest pocket. If I could ride as well as she does, I wouldn't need a rabbit's foot, thought Vicki.

Number three team peeled off and was on its way. They were going great guns, as a good team should; even, controlled, and really moving on. Vicki's eyes were on Lois, admiring the beautiful form that had won her the coveted Maclay Trophy at the Garden last year. Suddenly the girl's horse faltered and stumbled in the middle of the in-and-out. He tried desperately to regain his balance, but the force of his momentum propelled him headfirst into the second half of the structure. The ripping sound of splitting rails cut through the stillness as he came on over in a giant cartwheel and landed with a crash and explosion of dust so thick Vicki couldn't see a thing. The horror of the moment seemed to freeze everything in place — horses, riders, spectators. Then the ambulance was careening madly across the field toward the in-and-out. A gray pall of fog settled slowly around the demolished obstacle to reveal the horse flat and still — and nothing else. The two girls stared in horror.

"She's pinned under him," someone shouted.

The outcry broke the hush that had paralyzed the crowd. A black limousine skidded to a halt in front of their horses. A woman, whom Vicki recognized as Lois' mother, was helped in and they were off in the wake of

the ambulance. Down by the in-and-out, men were struggling to slide the unconscious girl out from under the fallen horse.

Vicki sat like a statue, unable to move a muscle. Suddenly her mouth was sandpaper, and a band of steel seemed wrapped around her middle, constricting her breathing. She still gripped Loli's reins, but her mind had blanked out — except for the picture of Lois kissing the rabbit's foot.

Mrs. Field came pushing her way between the two girls' horses. She reached up and gripped Kathy's knee. "Turn away, Kathy," she cried. "Turn away, don't look, you mustn't look." She was almost hysterical.

"Leave me alone, Mother — please leave me alone." Kathy was trying to pull free.

Dan Jordan edged his horse between mother and daughter. He leaned forward and placed his hand gently but firmly on Mrs. Field's shoulder. "Dorothy —— " his voice trembled — "leave the girl alone. Don't you think she's got enough to think about?"

Just then Mr. Field came striding up. He put his arm around his wife and led her away. Dan Jordan himself was shaken — shocked by what had just happened out there. He had been a soldier in the last war and had seen enough to be able to accept tragedy, but the girls had had little experience with this side of life. He understood what they were going through. He wanted to help but there was nothing he could say or do.

"Dad," Vicki's voice seemed to come from a great distance. "Aren't you frightened?"

"I sure am. I'm scared to death."

"Are we still going on?"

Mr. Jordan could see she was trying to master the creeping terror that threatened her.

"What do you want us to do Vicki, go home?"

Vicki pondered this for a moment before she answered. "No, we can't pull out now."

She heard somebody say the horse had broken his neck — Lois was on her way to the hospital. The loudspeaker announced there would be a twenty-minute delay before the class continued. But the joy of competition had vanished with the fading sunlight. The remaining teams stood quietly. Nobody had anything to say.

The minutes ticked away.

Herb Morris, the starter, walked up to Mr. Jordan. "Dan, will your team go next — sort of break the ice?"

Dan Jordan turned to the girls. "Well, what do you say, kids. Are we still a team?"

Vicki swallowed and nodded. Kathy's eyes said yes.

"Good," said Mr. Jordan.

"All right, ladies and gentlemen — the course is clear, start when you are ready."

"It's all yours, Vicki," Mr. Jordan murmured, "Let's take it away."

Now she was galloping on. The steady rhythm of Loli's hoofs brought her back to reality and the job ahead. The fences sped by smoothly, evenly. As she made the second turn she glanced back. Kathy was keeping her distance well and Pat, fifty yards behind Kathy, was holding steady. Vicki's fears vanished. Confidence rode with her once more over the white gate, through the in-and-out, and up the slope to the last fence. She could see Wayne and Mother and the Fields standing tensely by the aiken as Loli soared over it. When she pulled up her horse, Kathy came pounding up and stopped beside her — then Dad on Pat. Victory was in their eyes, but at this moment it didn't matter who won.

When the last team had finished, they sat at ease waiting for the judge's choice. After many minutes the loudspeaker rang out. "First place goes to team number eight."

"That's us," whispered Vicki. But nobody moved until the final award was announced. Then the steward came up and pinned blue ribbons to the browbands of the horses and handed neatly wrapped packages to each rider. A photographer took several pictures of them as they sat there three abreast. Vicki didn't feel the exhilaration she had thought she would. The falling horse, the crash and stillness that followed, the ambulance, Lois' mother; all these kept rushing and whirling through her mind. Even the applause seemed hushed.

Kathy went on home with her family. "I'll phone you tomorrow," she called to Vicki as they drove off.

When the horses were loaded, the Jordans drove slowly back to Random Farm. In the Jeep, Vicki rested her head against Wayne's shoulder. She didn't feel like talking. She felt drained and exhausted.

Jesse was overjoyed to see his roommate again. They rubbed noses between the bars — Pat seemed to be telling the pony all about his day.

And what a long day it had been, reflected Vicki. First the trailer coming loose, then the accident and the panic that had almost wrecked her.

At the house, when she was getting ready for sleep, she sat in her pajamas on the edge of the bed studying her yellow good-luck shirt. Finally she went to the doorway of her room.

"Mother," she called to Mrs. Jordan across the hall. "I think I'm going to put this yellow shirt in the box for the rummage sale. I'm getting too big for it."

8. The Gymkhana Meet

Lisa Watkins came over to school the Shetland one Sunday morning. She tacked up and led him across the road to the outdoor ring where they worked for almost an hour. She was a good little rider and in short order had Jesse bending in the corners and doing figure eights — even jumping a small fence.

Vicki hung over the top rail watching her enviously. She still didn't have a horse of her own to ride, and at such moments the longing became so intense, she had to walk away.

Dan Jordan studied her as she scuffed across the front lawn toward him. He was sitting on the front steps smoking his pipe. Vicki dropped down beside him and together they watched Lisa and the pony.

"What's the matter, honey?" he asked. But he knew. He knew by her face, her expression, her sigh as she cupped her chin in her hand. She shrugged but said nothing.

"He's a darn good mover for a pony," Mr. Jordan ventured. "Don't you think?"

Vicki nodded staring straight ahead.

"I'll bet you can get a pretty fair price for him — maybe enough to buy a pony or horse the right size for you."

This was no new thought to her, but it was the first time anyone had put it into words. Her first reaction was to say no, but she let his suggestion sink in and roll around a bit, without answering him.

Mr. Jordan knew he was treading on a touchy subject. He thought it would be better not to press her — to let her think about it. After all, Jesse was her pony.

Vicki got up and went into the house. Wayne was sprawled on the couch in the den reading the Sunday paper. Her mother was still in the kitchen finishing up the breakfast dishes. Vicki picked up a dish towel.

"Mom," she said, as she absent-mindedly wiped a frying pan. "Do you think I ought to sell Jesse?"

"It might be a good idea, but it's up to you, darling." Bette Jordan turned and studied Vicki's deep frown. She understood her daughter's mixed emotions.

"After all," she continued, "a pony should have someone to ride him. I know he can carry you — why he can even carry Daddy or me for a short distance, but we certainly wouldn't make a habit of riding him."

After the dishes were done Vicki strolled down to the barn. Jesse had already been put away and was standing quietly in his stall, chomping his hay. Pat's head was over his stall door and he nickered softly as she came through the doorway.

She put her face against his cheek and began scratching him between the eyes.

"What about it, Pat. What do you think?"

Pat nodded his head up and down but only to encourage the scratching — it felt so good.

Well, she wouldn't make any decisions now — at least not until after the gymkhana meet. Here most of the classes would consist of contests rather than regulation horse-show competitions. There would be sack races and relay races and pie-eating races — and a bunch of other crazy games. It would be a day of fun and horseplay that required a great deal of mounting and dismounting, so a pint-sized pony could prove very useful. The notice of the event that came yesterday said it would be held this coming Saturday on the Gibson place, about two miles away, which immediately eliminated the Jordans' vanning problems.

The night before the games, Vicki and Kathy pored over the program, trying to decide which classes they would enter. They were sprawled out on the rug in the Jordan library, the gymkhana program spread out between them. A two-dollar entry fee for each class governed the number they could compete in. There were several new classes this year — the egg race, the costume class, the balloon contest.

"What do you suppose the water race is, carrying a pot of water?" queried Kathy.

"On your head!" replied Vicki with a giggle. "And one in each hand and the reins in your teeth."

The girls laughed with delight at the thought of doing anything as silly as this. The could see horses and ponies running out of control, dumping their drenched riders in wild confusion.

"I really haven't the vaguest idea what a water race is," said Vicki when she could catch her breath again. "But we'll find out soon enough."

On Saturday morning Kathy came over after breakfast. She was dressed just like Vicki — in a shirt, jeans, and sneakers. Wayne wasn't taking the trip with them. He and some of his school chums were going to a tennis match in Westport. Kathy and Mrs. Jordan drove on ahead to the Gibson place. Dan Jordan and Vicki followed along on Pat and Jesse. The black horse really didn't belong in this kind of competition — he was too high-strung. But lately he had acted so disturbed every time he was separated from his pony friend, the Jordans decided to take him along.

On Dingle Ridge they met Mrs. Watkins on Loli and her daughter Lisa on Jeanie. They were on their way to the games too. Everyone was in a gay mood. Only the weather wasn't cooperating. The day was unseasonably cool and the sky was overcast, threatening to rain. But the way they felt now, nothing could dampen their high spirits.

At the corner of Vail's lane they ran into a party of six riders from the Maple Vista stable. They joined forces and moved along the dirt road like a cavalry patrol. Mrs. Jordan and Kathy met them at the entrance to the Gibson estate.

"Hurry up, Vick," she called. "I've entered you and Kathy in the relay race — they're almost ready to begin now!"

The loudspeaker was bellowing forth the announcement. "Relay race coming up. Open to riders under sixteen. Teams will be assembled in the ring — get your numbers."

"There will be four riders to one pony," the announcer's voice sang out. "At the whistle, rider number one will mount and make one complete lap around the ring track. Number two takes the next trip and so on until the last rider has gone."

The rules of the race were repeated several times while the teams were being organized. Vicki knew Jesse was fast and responsive, their chances looked good. Kathy would start off on the pony, Peter Nichols was number two, Cynthia Carpenter from Eight Bells Farm was number three, and Vicki would ride fourth — to victory she hoped.

There were nine ponies in the line-up. Mrs. Jordan was at ringside chatting quietly with Kathy's mother who was nervously twisting her handkerchief into a knot. Mr. Jordan was in the ring coaching Vicki's team.

"Dismount on the right side so your teammate can be mounting at the same time — that way you won't waste precious seconds."

Finally the teams were all set. The starter had his arm raised. Jesse was steady and calm, undisturbed by the hubbub. Peter Nichols was crouched down beside Kathy, whose left knee was bent and cradled in his hands. Her fingers gripped Jesse's mane, her body curved forward tense with anticipation — eager to be lifted atop the pony and on her way.

At the whistle blast Peter lifted so hard he tossed Kathy completely over Jesse's back. She landed in the arms of her teammates who quickly hoisted her up to where she belonged. Vicki stepped back, whacked Jesse smartly across the rump, and amidst wild cheers the race was on.

Advice of all kinds was being screamed from both sides of the arena.

"Mike, use your legs — more — more — more!"

"Give him his head!"

"Let him go!"

As each successive rider made his round, the shouts and cries of the spectators grew louder and louder. Cynthia, number three, was galloping toward Vicki now. Their team was in the lead. Jesse's mane and tail were streaming behind as if he were on fire.

"Hurry Cynthia, faster — faster!"

Jesse came sliding in like a polo pony. Cynthia was off his back almost before he came to a halt.

"He's all yours, Vick!"

Vicki scrambled to her pony's back as he dug in for his final run. She was too anxious, too much in a hurry. She misjudged and landed on the pony's rump. Frantically she reached for his mane in a last-ditch effort to pull herself into position, but her clutching fingers got a handful of air instead. As if someone had lit a firecracker under

his tail, Jesse dropped his head and kicked up his hind-quarters. That first buck put Vicki astride his neck, the second pointed her wildly thrashing legs to the heavens. She came to earth on her backside as Jesse and the other ponies shot past in a shower of dust and flying hunks of dirt. She rolled to her elbows and watched with disgust as they raced around and down the home stretch. Jesse

crossed the finish line first — but a riderless pony is automatically disqualified.

Mr. Jordan hopped on Jeanie for the next event which was for adults only. This was the egg race and the loudspeaker supplied the rules.

"Each contestant will be given a spoon. Race your horse to the far end of the ring. There an egg will be placed on the spoon. Turn and get back to where you started and drop the egg in the basket. First one in is the winner."

At the whistle seven riders mounted on ponies and small horses galloped down the length of the ring. Mr. Jordan picked up his egg, turned, and was heading back. Vicki and Kathy were screaming and jumping up and down madly. Suddenly the egg popped off his spoon and rolled on the grass without breaking. Mr. Jordan quickly slipped to the ground, retrieved the egg and, clutching it in his fingers, vaulted back on Jeanie. He came in last and slid to a halt in front of his family. He was grinning broadly and holding aloft his hand which was dripping yellow egg yolk.

"Someone forgot to hard-boil this one." He laughed.

Bette Jordan with Loli entered the bareback balloon contest for ladies only. There were sixteen entries. A balloon was attached by a long string to the waist of each rider.

"At the whistle, break any balloon you can reach — the last one left is the winner."

The whistle blew and pandemonium broke loose. The first balloon that burst under Loli's nose put Mrs. Jordan on the ground so fast she landed on her feet with the reins still in her hand. She remounted and joined the fracas once more. Pop! Bang! Bang! Mrs. Broad hit the ground next, then Mrs. Jordan again right on top of her. Everyone was laughing so hard, sometimes Vicki could barely hear the popping balloons. But Loli heard them, every one —

and without a saddle to help, Mrs. Jordan didn't have a chance. She was on the ground more often than on Loli's back. Yet somehow, through all this, her balloon remained intact. Mrs. Broad and Mrs. Jordan were the last ones left, battling away like a couple of gladiators. Once Vicki heard a ripping sound as her mother's jacket parted up the middle of the back and hung in two sections from her shoulders. It flapped like a pair of wings as she wheeled and twisted, trying to get at or escape from her opponent.

The judge finally called it a draw and awarded a blue ribbon and a bottle of champagne to each. As the exhausted women left the ring, a great cheer followed them to the refreshment stand.

They dismounted and ordered Cokes just as the noon break was called. Mrs. Field lent Mrs. Jordan a sweater to replace the torn jacket — for the day was growing cooler by the minute. They had soft drinks and hamburgers for lunch, and Kathy's mother had brought delicious apple pie. They ate quickly. The afternoon go-round had already begun.

It began to drizzle, but the games went on: wrestling contest — sack race — barrel race. Mr. Broad got bucked off during the costume race and Kathy fell off Jeanie during the under-sixteen jumping class. Then Lisa entered the same class on Jeanie and won it. There was a bareback jumping class for adults which Mr. Jordan on Pat almost won until he went off course and got himself disqualified.

Vicki and Jesse entered the last event on the program, the water race. Kathy joined the sidelines cheering section with her mother and the Jordans.

The riders on their ponies lined up in the center ring. A small empty bucket was placed on the grass in front of each pony. A smaller one was given to each rider. The announcer outlined what would be required.

"At the starting signal you will ride to the large tub of water at the end of the ring, fill the pail you are carrying, then return as fast as you can and start filling your bucket in ring center. You do not have to dismount if you don't want to — but you must completely fill the bucket in the ring in order to qualify. The first one whose bucket is filled is the winner."

Jesse was the smallest pony in the competition. This was a handicap where speed was concerned, but it also gave Vicki an advantage which showed up about ten seconds after the starting signal. She and Jesse reached the tub several strides behind the other contestants who were floundering about trying to fill their pails as quickly as possible. Most of them had to dismount to do this, then try to remount their excited ponies without spilling too much water. But Vicki rode Jesse up against the tank, leaned sideways, filled her pail with one scoop — wheeled and raced back to ring center.

There again she stayed right in the saddle — just reached down and gently poured her water into the bucket. Bedlam was all around her. Ponies were knocking over buckets, one stepped through his. Because the riders on the larger ponies had to dismount at both ends of the line, it put them out of the running almost immediately.

Jesse did his job in a steady, unruffled manner that brought cheers of approval from the spectators. Vicki made only five trips to fill her bucket and won an undisputed victory. Nobody was even close.

After they were pinned, and with her trophy cradled in her arms, Vicki proudly guided her pony toward the outgate. The Jordans and the Fields gathered about, congratulating her. Mr. Broad pushed his way through the crowd.

"That's a great pony you've got there," he said. "He really showed them, didn't he? Nothing bothered him, just went right ahead and did his job."

Dan Jordan agreed. "He's got the temperament all right. Too bad he's so small."

"Joe Shroyer is always looking for this kind, Dan. Ever think of selling him?"

Vicki, still on the pony's back was watching her dad's face — waiting. She knew about the Shroyer pony farm, and even though she had considered this she had never said a word about it to anyone.

Dan Jordan's eyes were on Vicki but his words were directed to Mr. Broad. "Why don't you have Joe call me this evening if he's interested," he said casually. "We might be able to do business."

At the dinner table, school was the main topic of conversation, for the summer vacation was about to end.

"If you think eighth grade was tough," predicted

Wayne, "wait till you get into ninth." His expression was pained as if someone had punched him in the stomach. "You may as well say good-bye to your horses, little girl; with all that homework you'll never get a chance to ride again."

"Oh, stop it, Wayne," scolded Mrs. Jordan. "Stop teasing your sister, and pass the butter, please."

Vicki was barely listening anyway. Her mind was on the phone call which hadn't come yet. She ate her dinner mechanically, preoccupied with her thoughts and indecisions. She had almost finished her apple pie when the jangling phone nearly jolted her out of the chair. Her dad got up to answer it.

"Why, yes, Joe — sure — she's right here, why don't you ask her?"

Vicki rose quietly. Mr. Jordan smiled encouragingly as he handed her the phone.

"It's Mr. Shroyer."

"Hello, Mr. Shroyer."

"Good evening, Vicki." His voice sounded as if it came from the next room. "I'd like to come over and take a look at that pony of yours." Then he added quickly, "He's for sale, isn't he?"

Answer the man. Her mind was going a mile a minute as she told herself, "Don't just stand there — is he for sale or isn't he?" She didn't know whether she was stalling because she wanted Jesse so much or because she knew he got along so well with Pat. Would another pony make Pat as happy as Jesse did? But after all she did want a pony she could ride and Jesse was too small.

"Are you there?" came Mr. Shroyer's persistent voice.

Vicki gripped the phone harder. "I'm here," she answered weakly.

"*Is* your pony for sale, Vicki?"

"I guess so — yes, Mr. Shroyer, he's for sale."

9. Good-bye to Jesse

The sun breaking through the overcast sky spotlighted the pony, the girl, and the two men in the barnyard. The past four months with the Jordans had brought about a remarkable change in his appearance. There wasn't a jagged edge left on him. He was a pony again; round, stocky, proud, and right now extremely alert listening to Pat's whinny which came from the barn with clock-like regularity.

When he answered, his whole body vibrated right down to the end of his halter shank which Vicki held uncertainly. She tried to concentrate on Jesse but she kept looking over to her dad and Mr. Shroyer. He was leaning back against the barnyard fence. He reminded her of one of the characters she had seen on a TV Western the other night — wide-brimmed hat, leathery face, knotty brown hands with thumbs hooked in belt, even to the frontier pants and high-heeled boots.

Mr. Shroyer was studying the pony, trying to decide what to offer, but at this moment Vicki still wasn't sure she wanted to sell. The idea of giving Jesse up was almost too much to bear. But then again she had never been able to part with anything. Toys, dolls, trinkets, and gadgets she had accumulated over her thirteen years lined every available space in her room.

Then Vicki heard Mr. Shroyer say, "I'll give you a hundred and fifty dollars for him." That sounded pretty good. She glanced at her dad.

"Oh, come on, Joe, you can do better than that." Then to Vicki, he said, "Trot him out, honey, show Mr. Shroyer how this pony can move."

Vicki did as she was told.

"Look at him go, Joe. He'll make some kid a fine hunting pony. He can keep up with any horse in the field."

Mr. Shroyer considered this. He grinned broadly as Vicki stopped Jesse in front of him. She was panting from the exertion of running around the barnyard.

"OK, Vicki." He roughed up her windblown hair. "That run was worth twenty-five dollars more. A hundred and seventy-five dollars, how's that? You might buy something real good for that money this time of year."

She nodded — she couldn't trust her voice yet.

"I'll send the trailer down for him this afternoon or to-morrow."

He and Mr. Jordan walked toward his car parked in the driveway.

Vicki led Jesse back to his stall. He and Pat touched noses through the bars.

She hung up the halter shank and walked slowly back

to the house. Her throat was tight and her chest felt constricted. Her eyes kept blinking rapidly, trying to hold back the tears.

Early the following morning Vicki watched Jesse leave Random Farm in a horse trailer. When the tail gate was hooked up, only his ears and the top of his forelock were visible. He began whinnying the moment the trailer start-

ed out down the drive. The morning stillness was shattered again and again and again by his frantic bellowing calls. And Pat's answering whinny was so high, so persistent that Vicki shut herself in the cellar with her hands pressed tightly against her ears, trying to block out the heart-rending sound.

When she ventured forth again, Jesse was gone. Silence had spread over the barnyard. Even the geese and ducks had nothing to say as she walked between them. Teddy was poised at the end of his rope gazing down Dingle Ridge where Jesse had gone and Rocky was sitting in the middle of the road gazing off in the same direction. Across the way Loli, the Watkins' mare, was very alert — frozen in a startled hush — like Jeanie standing tensely beside her.

In the barn, Pat was pacing about his stall as if he were a mare who had just been separated from her foal. He didn't even glance in Vicki's direction as she rested her arms on the top of his stall door. He had stopped whinnying. Every once in a while he would halt and listen, his ears and nostrils straining the air for the slightest clue to his buddy's whereabouts. When his eyes did find Vicki they seemed filled with accusation. She opened his door and put her arms around his neck — pressed her face against it. But Pat paid no attention to her — he didn't even seem to know she was there.

The school bus horn was honking. Vicki rushed out of the barn and ran madly toward the road where the big yellow bus was waiting. She had almost forgotten this was

the first day of school. Wayne was standing in the doorway of the bus yelling, "Hurry, hurry, hurry!"

Buzz, the driver, laughed as she came panting up.
"Take it easy, girl. We won't leave without you."

It was good to see Buzz again with his big good-
humored grin and that familiar leather jacket. Kathy was
sitting about halfway back saving a seat. Vicki half-
heartedly acknowledged the greetings of her classmates
as she followed Wayne down the aisle and slid in beside
her friend.

"How do you like my new dress, Vick?" Kathy asked as
she smoothed the front of her crisp blue skirt.

"It's beautiful," Vicki answered quickly but her eyes
were focused on the road up ahead — the way the trailer
had gone.

The bus reached Route 121, then turned into Bloomerside Road. They were almost at school when Shroyer's
trailer appeared in front of them. She could see Jesse inside — the wind grabbing at his shaggy mane as the
vehicle bounced along the bumpy road.

"That's Jesse!" exclaimed Kathy.

Vicki nodded and her eyes filled with tears.

At the corner of Route 124, the bus stopped for another
pickup. The trailer swung left. The girls watched as it
moved ahead and disappeared around the bend. Neither
spoke. Kathy slipped her arm around Vicki's shoulder.

10. The Search Begins

"He'll get over it — inside of one week he'll forget he ever knew that pony!"

Dan Jordan was consoling his daughter. She was fretting about Pat again. Why didn't he stop carrying on like this? He had been leaving his grain for three days now — ever since Jesse went away. All he did was pace back and forth or paw holes in the floor of his stall. And in his pasture he barely grazed, just galloped along the fence, whinnying constantly until he was lathered with sweat.

Vicki was worried — much more than her dad. She knew he was worried too, though he kept telling her things were going to be all right, and that Pat would get over it.

But what if he didn't get over it? Horses and ponies had been separated before. There was always a slight upheaval but things usually simmered down in a day or so. Vicki knew this, she had seen it happen — then why not Pat? Was he so different?

"You can't account for these things," Dad always said.

"Horses are like people — each has his own personality."

Maybe Jesse meant more to Pat than the Jordans ever guessed. But whatever the case might be there wasn't much anybody could do about it right now — or was there?

Vicki vaguely considered this two weeks after Jesse's departure. She was sitting with Kathy on the gate at the south end of the lower pasture watching Pat moving restlessly along the fence. Both girls had just returned from their weekly tennis lesson.

"Isn't he just the handsomest thing you ever saw?" Kathy declared with a sigh.

"Not now he isn't," Vicki answered without taking her eyes off Pat.

"Oh, you're crazy, Vick. Julie Horgan thinks he's beautiful too!"

"How would Julie know? She's never even seen him."

"What do you mean she's never seen him?" Kathy was perplexed. "She was there with us today."

Vicki straightened up, annoyed. She looked straight into Kathy's blue eyes. "What in the world are you talking about?"

"Steve Ratchford, our tennis instructor, of course!"

Vicki blew out her breath and turned her eyes back to Pat. "Oh, Kathy, I was talking about Pat."

Kathy snorted and brushed her blonde hair back from her pretty face. "Honestly, Vicki, that's all you ever seem to talk about — Pat this and Pat that. I love horses too, but you don't hear me going on about them all day. You'd think Pat was all that mattered in the world."

"He is," Vicki thought. "I'm sorry," she said. "I guess I am being a bore about Pat. But look at him, he's lost about twenty-five pounds since Jesse left. Look at his flanks, all tucked up, and his coat looks so dull and awful. Gosh, Kathy, I don't know what to do."

Kathy's rising temper vanished completely and she moved closer to her friend. For almost two minutes neither spoke as each one wrestled with Pat's problem. Suddenly Kathy leaped down from the gate and faced Vicki.

"I've got it!" Her voice was animated with discovery. "Why don't you buy Jesse back — you still have the money, haven't you?"

Vicki nodded listlessly. She still had the money — in her bank account in Granville. Since the sale of Jesse she had had two opportunities to buy a horse. She told herself they weren't her kind, which wasn't exactly true. One of them, a blue roan gelding, would have suited fine. He was young with good temperament and a wonderful jumper, but something inside made her hang back. She had been half thinking of buying Jesse back, but kept stalling, hoping Pat would forget about him. And even though he hadn't so far, she still could not come to a decision. But then decisions were always difficult for Vicki. She couldn't make up her mind about anything — except of course the way she felt about Pat. She loved him. He was her friend, her companion, and now he was unhappy. It was her fault too, for if she had not bought Jesse in the first place this would never have happened.

She sat up straighter. "Kathy, you're right! Of course I'll buy him back — that's what I'll do. Pat wants his friend Jesse and, by gosh, Pat's going to get him!"

She hopped off the gate and began striding rapidly toward Dingle Ridge. Kathy had to trot to keep up.

"Vicki," she puffed. "Where are we going?"

"To Shroyer's pony farm," Vicki announced without slowing down.

Shroyer's pony farm lay in a long valley almost two miles from the Jordans'. Though the sun still shone as the two girls passed beneath the wooden archway that bridged the drive, off to the west the sky was darkened to a purple hue. The distant low rumble of thunder heralded an approaching storm. The post and rail along both sides of the roadway bordered a series of pastures. Ordinarily the girls would stop and talk with the numerous pony mares and colts that came up at a gallop to see who the visitors were. But today they had no time to dally around.

The horsehoe knocker sounded too loud when Vicki banged it once aganst the door of the small frame house. Mrs. Shroyer opened it. She was wiping her hands on a blue apron and smiled pleasantly when she recognized Vicki and Kathy.

"Goodness sakes, you two girls look as though you've been running — come in, come in." She shut the door behind them. "Looks like we're going to have some rain. Heavens to Betsy, we can use it — my petunias are simply drying up."

The two girls stood awkwardly in the living room. Now that she was here, Vicki didn't quite know what to say — how to begin.

"How would you girls like some ice-cold lemonade and some brownies just out of the oven?"

Without waiting for an answer, Mrs. Shroyer turned toward the kitchen from which issued the most delicious smells.

The room they were in was lined with many photographs of ponies and riders and quite a few jumping pictures. A glass cabinet next to the TV was filled with silver trophies of all sizes and shapes. The flower-patterned chairs looked inviting after their long hot walk but neither of the girls made a move to sit down.

"Hello Vicki, come to sell me another pony?"

Mr. Shroyer was standing in the doorway of the hall — he must have come in quietly through the side entrance. He hung his Stetson on the coat rack and, mopping his brow with a red kerchief, grunted as he sank down into a big easy chair. He was smiling. He looked much friendlier than the day he had bought Jesse.

"Mr. Shroyer," Vicki began.

He was stuffing tobacco into his pipe now — absorbed in it. Mrs. Shroyer came in carrying a tray with the brownies and lemonade. The roll of thunder was closer.

Vicki now held a glass of lemonade in one hand and a brownie in the other.

"Thank you," she said almost under her breath.

"Mr. Shroyer," she tried again, and with conviction, "I've come to buy Jesse back!"

Mr. Shroyer's lighted match hung poised over his pipe bowl. "Why would you want to do that, Vicki?" His voice was gentle.

"Because Pat misses him so — I've got to get him back for Pat."

"And who's Pat?"

"He's my horse — I mean Dad's horse. He has stopped eating and he looks awful!"

"Your dad?"

"No — Pat!"

"Maybe he needs a good worming."

"I don't think so, Mr. Shroyer. Our vet doesn't think there's anything wrong with him. He just needs Jesse."

Mr. Shroyer rose, walked to the window and shut it. A breeze was coming up. Vicki could hear the leaves beginning to rustle — warming up for a big blow.

"I don't have your pony any more." Mr. Shroyer's words came out as if he hated to speak them. Vicki's heart dropped down to her shoes as the full meaning of what he had said registered. For a moment she felt weak in the knees and sat down.

"I'm awfully sorry Vicki, but I sold your pony just about a week ago. Fellow came along, said he was looking for something suitable for pony rides. He bought your pony and a couple of others that wouldn't show. Let me see now, I think he was taking them over to the fair at Carmel."

Vicki sat stiffly, gripping the glass of lemonade. Her eyes were fastened to the rug.

Joe Shroyer strode across the room to the hallway and lifted his hat off the rack. "Come on girls, I'll drive you over to Carmel. See if we can find this pony of yours."

Vicki almost wanted to kiss him.

They were approaching Carmel when the first drops pelted the windshield.

"Looks like we're gonna get a good one!!" Mr. Shroyer commented. These were the first words spoken since they left the pony farm twenty minutes ago. Kathy sat in the middle and Vicki on the outside. Her eyes were on the road — her hands twisting nervously in the folds of her tennis skirt.

"Here we are." Mr. Shroyer braked to a halt alongside a billboard that announced the Carmel Fair. Vicki was out almost before the car stopped.

The field was empty. There were no tents, no ferris wheel, no roller coaster. The fair had come and gone. The wind and swirls of dust were steadily increasing. Paper cups rolled about and newspapers, like crippled white birds, were whipping across the land — one newspaper slapped against Vicki's leg, then twisted free and flew on.

The three of them stood as if they had turned to stone — staring at the approaching storm. Mr. Shroyer moved first.

"We'd better get out of here — girls, let's move on!"

There was no more reference made to Jesse as Mr. Shroyer drove back. At the Jordan place he stopped to let the girls out. They dashed quickly across the lawn toward

the house, for the rain was beginning to move in. A giant clap of thunder propelled them both through the doorway as the storm broke in wild fury.

As she ran up the stairs to her room Vicki remembered she hadn't thanked Mr. Shroyer. The two girls pressed against the window, watching the mulberry tree sway and groan before the onslaught of the wind. Through the wild, waving branches they could see Pat beneath them in the pasture, oblivious to the lightning and crashing thunder. His mane snapped along the crest of his neck like black fire. His tail was crushed against his quarters and up under his belly. He could have run to the barn if he'd wished but he didn't move — didn't seem to care.

"He *does* look awful!" Kathy spoke hardly above a whisper.

Suddenly the wind shifted and a sheet of water smashed against the windowpane, drowning out the tree and the pasture and the black horse standing alone.

11. The Auction

The beginning of the school year hardly slowed down Vicki's search for Jesse. She wouldn't give up. She felt she would be letting Pat down if she did. The man who bought Jesse had signed the bill of sale with an illegible scrawl that looked like Petingale or Pasternak. Anyway, neither she nor her dad could find any trace of him. It wouldn't have mattered much, for he had probably resold Jesse. That was the way many dealers operated — buy, sell, swap — till the end caught up with the beginning and he could wind up buying his own pony and never know the difference.

Mr. Shroyer felt badly about what had happened and offered a pony to take Jesse's place.

"Take him home on trial — see how the black horse likes him."

The replacement was small and squat and gray, almost Jesse's size. He had a great deal of appeal the Jordans thought — only Pat didn't agree. First he ignored the little thing, then turned on him with his ears flat back and his teeth bared.

The pony stayed around almost a week but, if Pat didn't want to have anything to do with him, there was no sense keeping him. He went back to the Shroyer place.

The Maple Vista stable sent over one of theirs, but it flopped just as badly.

Vicki renewed her hunt for Jesse with new vigor — and Kathy's help. Together they began a systematic search of the stables within a twenty-mile radius. After school, and on weekends, with Wayne behind the wheel of the station wagon they combed the area like a couple of "private eyes" hoping to find some tiny clue that might lead them to Jesse.

Nobody had seen him. Only once their hopes were raised when someone they asked said, "Oh yeah — Mike Girkus down Yorktown way picked up a couple of ponies last week. I think one of them was a Shetland, not sure though." But when they got to Yorktown, not only was Jesse not there but Mike Girkus didn't have a pony on the place. As a matter of fact, he didn't even know what they were talking about.

Nothing would make Vicki stop her search. Her mother had never seen her so determined. Her mind became one track, pointing toward one goal. Her school work suffered, but Mrs. Jordan knew this was something Vicki had to do. The whole family pitched in to help whenever they could. Even Wayne stopped teasing her about her softheartedness. He was very patient these days and understanding.

It was October now. The leaves were turning red and

gold, drifting earthward to cover the green grass like a patchwork quilt of bright color. The fox-hunting season had begun, but Dan Jordan rode the Watkins' mare Loli — not Pat.

The black horse had fallen off badly. After a while Dr. Regan thought maybe a worming might help, but Pat's condition remained the same.

"It's hard to believe that Jesse is the cause of all this," Dan Jordan said at the dinner table one evening. "I've been around horses all my life. If anyone ever told me a horse would pine away for a pony, I'd say they didn't know what they were talking about. But that's what seems to be happening to Pat. He looks like the devil, but Doc Regan says he can't find a thing wrong with him. The horse just doesn't seem to give a hoot any more — all his spirit seems to have gone out of him.

"Yesterday I jumped him over a couple of fences back of the Murdock place. He practically fell on his face as if he didn't know they were there." Dan Jordan stopped and looked directly at his wife. "To be honest with you, right now I'd be afraid to take him out in the hunting field — might kill both of us. Beats me — never heard of anything like it."

Later that evening, Vicki went down to the barn to give Pat some carrots. He was standing dejectedly in his stall with his back to the door.

"Hi, Black Horse, how about a big kiss?"

Her forced cheerfulness didn't even twitch his ear. She walked in and began stroking his neck. He mouthed the carrots a bit, then became preoccupied again. His feed was barely touched. How long could this go on?

Back at the house Wayne called out from the den. "Hey, Vicki, I just read there's a horse and pony auction up in Pawling tomorrow afternoon. Let's go and have a look — you can never tell."

Saturday afternoon was hot — much too hot for October. Vicki and Wayne sat in the front row of the indoor amphitheater where the auction was being held. It reminded her of a small-town southern courtroom she had once seen in a movie, only here, in place of the judge, sat the auctioneer. There must have been over three hundred men, women, and children, closely packed, fanning themselves, waiting for the auction to begin.

The first horse was led in quietly. Suddenly the auctioneer's chant blasted off like a machine gun and was magnified by the loudspeaker into a staccato barrage of ear-splitting sound.

Vicki couldn't make head or tail of the mumbo jumbo of words. It was a foreign language to her. Now and again she could catch a word or number, but for the most part she couldn't make sense out of any of it.

Only the sad-looking creature standing forlornly on the wood-shaving-covered floor had meaning to her. He was a raw-boned bay, Number 909 plastered to his left hip. He was terribly thin but a heavy western stock saddle was draped over the middle of him covering a multitude of ribs and neglect. A thin sharp-faced fellow in jeans, his shirttail hanging out, swung to his back and began show-

ing him off to the prospective buyers. The space was hardly larger than a good-sized box stall but the rider somehow managed to neck-rein the horse into tight figure eights demonstrating his handiness. A man who looked exactly like a weasel stood by with a whip flicking it constantly to keep the horse animated.

The rattle of the auctioneer and the snapping whip mesmerized Vicki — held her rapt and immovable — feeling there was something she should do but didn't know what.

This horse was sold for seventy dollars. The next for fifty-eight, then forty — everything cheap, under a hundred dollars. Each creature was as awful-looking as the next — some even had sores on their backs.

What hurt her deeply was the utter resignation of these beasts. They were spiritless. They didn't care — because nobody else did. She wished she could buy every one — to take home and turn out in green pastures. But she was helpless and sick. Her fingers dug into Wayne's arm. After the horses would come the ponies. If they had arrived earlier they could have gone through the stockyards to see if Jesse was there. Now all she could do was sit and suffer and wait as the auctioneer wrangled on and on.

The ponies were in better flesh than the horses. They were hardier and fared better under adverse conditions. The last on the auction floor was a tiny spotted pony foal, five months old. He was pathetic-looking — resembling a newborn calf with large frightened eyes and dirt-crusted coat. Vicki's heart melted immediately. She almost forgot that she had come to try to find Jesse.

"Let's buy him, Wayne!" She gripped his arm tighter, eagerly. "Please let's buy him, Wayne!"

"Vick, we can't buy him, you forget what we're here for!"

"But look at him, he's so sad and alone. He was probably just weaned — he's still looking for his mother."

At this point the foal let go with a shrill high-pitched whinny. It tore at her insides but the auctioneer's voice drowned out the sound. Abruptly the bidding was at an end.

"Sold for thirty-five dollars!"

Vicki moaned. Wayne took her arm and together they wended their way through the crush to the outdoors. He led her quickly to the station wagon. She flopped into the front seat with her head thrown back against the headrest. Her eyes were shut tight.

Once on the road, Wayne said, "I'm sorry Vick, but we just couldn't buy that foal — you know we couldn't. Dad would raise the roof if we came back with another pony and that one wouldn't do Pat any good."

They arrived home at five o'clock. The ducks and geese were gathered on the front lawn, squawking and honking to beat the band. "I'm hungry, I'm hungry."

There was no one about. Wayne went into the house and Vicki headed for the barn with a wedge formation of quacking creatures fanning out behind her. The chickens joined in and the bantams. She was hardly aware of them, for her mind was still occupied with the auction. Automatically she fed and watered them until the racket simmered down.

Now to feed Pat. His stall was empty and he wasn't in his pasture. Maybe Dad was out for a late ride.

She saw her dad's car coming up the barn drive. He got out and Mom followed. There was a curious distraught look about them.

Vicki's heart sank. Her stomach gave a funny upward jerk. Something had happened — something was wrong.

"Dad, what's happened, where's Pat?"

Dan Jordan answered slowly, puzzled. "He got out this afternoon — we can't find him anywhere." Then he quickly added, "Don't worry, you can't lose a horse in this country — especially a black one."

This was the last straw, the final blow that left Vicki numb — and at last discouraged.

12. The Swamp

That night the thermometer dropped twenty degrees — from seventy to fifty. Sunday morning dawned bleak and blustery with the threat of an early winter. Vicki woke when it was barely light and even though her dad had reported Pat's disappearance to the local police, she wanted to go out searching. She would never forgive herself if anything happened to him. She was convinced Pat had gone off in search of Jesse. He had never left like this before. Perhaps in his own way he felt that if the Jordans couldn't find Jesse, he could. But as Wayne said, it made more sense to stay at home to get messages or phone calls.

There were three calls around eleven — all false alarms. Each time the phone rang, Vicki's hopes soared skyward, hung suspended for an instant, then crashed to earth leaving her weak and trembling and worse off than she was before. She visualized Pat lying crippled in some lonely out-of-the-way place or trapped in a bog struggling in slimy filth. Her imagination was running out of control

— torturing her and tearing her apart. To escape her restlessness she made frequent trips to the barn, half hoping Pat might have come back. Once as she stood in his stall she thought she heard him walking in from the pasture, but it was only loose shale sliding down the slope beside the barn.

"Oh Pat, come back, please come back."

A jangling ring interrupted her thoughts. She leaped for the phone in the tackroom. Mr. Jordan picked it up at the house.

"Hello, Dan, this is Dick Bandler down at headquarters. We got a report from Fox Run Farm that a black horse got in with their racing stock last night. The description sounds like your Pat, especially the white hairs at the base of his tail."

Vicki hung up and raced to the house. Her dad called the farm.

It was Pat all right — he was in a stall now and could be picked up anytime.

Dan Jordan knew what his daughter had gone through these past hours. The constant pain and self-accusation in her eyes had disturbed him more than he would admit. Now as she stood beside him he could sense her great relief and suddenly, spontaneously, he said, "Honey, you can ride Pat home if you like."

As if he had presented her with a trip to the moon, her eyes widened and her mouth opened, then clamped shut. She swallowed hard.

"You mean I can ride Pat back by myself?"

"If you want to."

"Want to!" Vicki was bursting with delight. "I'd love to Daddy — Oh, I'd love to!"

At three-thirty that afternoon, Mr. Jordan drove Vicki to Fox Run Farm. As they bumped along the dirt road, Vicki slumped back comfortably with Pat's saddle on her lap and his bridle slung over her shoulder. She was temporarily at peace with herself and the world.

"I am actually going to ride Pat."

She smiled at the anticipation of her coming journey, for to Vicki this would be the greatest thing that could ever happen — a momentous occasion to be treasured forever.

The station wagon passed between the two hobbyhorses that marked the entrance to Fox Run Farm. Up ahead she could see the big red barns which lay just to the north of the main house. As her dad slowed to a halt, Jim Agate, the superintendent, came out of his office. He was a smooth-shaven man, slim and good-humored.

"Looks like that black horse of yours wants to get back into the racing business." He smiled, then led the way into the stable and down the runway between the stalls.

Vicki loved this place. She had been here twice before to visit the mares and the foals who would some day race on tracks all over the country. She always got a peculiar thrill when she petted a yearling colt or two-year-old and thought, this may be a great race horse — some day this colt may stand in the winner's circle at Churchill Downs with a garland of roses around his neck and thousands of people cheering his victory.

"Here is your run-away," said Jim Agate.

Pat was standing in a stall at the end of the line. His head was over the door. He nickered softly as Vicki came up to him.

"You're a bad boy — running off and giving us such an awful fright."

She scratched his nose, then opened the door and quickly slipped the snaffle bridle over his head. He took the bit readily as he always did and she led him out on the corridor floor. Her dad slid the saddle into place and girthed it up snugly. He gave Vicki a leg up. She rose to the saddle like a bird and settled into the curved leather seat.

It felt wonderful up here on top of the black horse. She gazed about her, marveling at her newly acquired elevation. She had never seen Pat's head from this position. His neck seemed so long and his small, curvy ears so far away. The feel of him against her legs was solid and warm as she had always known it would be. He moved lightly toward the open barn door and the soft click of his steel-shod hoofs rapped against the wood-plank floor like a far-off distant drum beat.

Outside she zipped up her jacket — squirmed into her riding gloves. Dad was talking horses with Mr. Agate. He looked up at Vicki. "All set, honey?"

She nodded. "We'll cut cross country to Bloomerside

Road — should be home in an hour."

"Look," cried Mr. Agate, pointing upward.

Vicki glanced in that direction. Way up there, below the gray overcast, a V formation of Canadian geese was heading south, honking. It was a thrilling sight to behold but she shivered — winter was on its way.

Her dad got back into the car and Vicki turned Pat north up an old cow path. Just ahead the high-tension wires crossed fifty feet above. She turned left to follow along beneath, for she knew they eventually crossed Bloomerside Road. The terrain dipped steeply in front of her. Vicki sat back relaxed, letting Pat pick his way down. At the bottom of a wide gully the overhead cables swung right. If she had been more alert, she would have been forewarned by the tall bunch grass and fernlike plants that a swamp lay ahead. If Pat were himself, he too would have become instantly suspicious of the look of things. Instead, they moved slowly ahead through the tall greenery, unsuspecting.

Vicki slammed against Pat's neck as the earth gave way beneath him. He heaved upward, trying to regain his footing, then went down again. She left the saddle head-first and struck the swamp on her hands. Pat was above her, floundering like a great seal. She rolled clear as the black horse surged ahead — fighting to get his legs under him — going down and coming up, then down again. He lay where he fell wheezing — sucking air in short whistling gasps. Vicki slogged through the mire to his head. She gripped the slippery reins and jerked him to his feet.

He plunged forward, then bogged down, sinking. This time he rolled to his side. Black muck was running off his shoulder and flanks. He lay still for a moment with his head raised, breathing heavily. Vicki reached his side and loosened his girth. Terror gripped her, but she knew she must not panic. "Let him catch his wind — keep calm." His eyes were on hers, strangely quiet.

Seeing Pat lying there helpless completely unnerved her. She began trembling and her teeth chattered with the cold.

Wild, hysterical thoughts rushed madly through her brain — threatening her self-control. She crouched down in the mud beside him and pressed her face into his neck. She could feel the throbbing beat of his pulse. Above, the gray sky darkened and the bare distorted shapes of the woods seemed to close in like an army of witches ready to pounce.

"Please, Pat," she pleaded, "you've rested long enough. Please — try to get up."

She pulled on his reins. His neck stretched forward but his body didn't move. Maybe he had broken a leg — what if he had ruptured an intestine and was bleeding internally right now? She looked about her. A fine mist was falling. Only Pat's labored breathing broke the stillness. "Help! Help! Help me! Someone help me!" But no one heard. It was as if they were the only two things left alive in the whole world.

In desperation she broke off the branch of a tree. She brought the switch down with all her might across Pat's

rump. Startled, he struggled to his feet and tottered upright on a rotten log and stood balanced there as if he were a performing circus animal. He was blacker than black, including the saddle. Chunks of mud dripped from his chin and belly. Blood seeped from his lacerated knees.

Vicki moved forward, trying to feel the consistency of the bottom, Pat followed. Unfortunately, what held her up would not support him. Twice more he fell. Each time she let him rest, then urged him to his feet and went on again. They turned east toward higher ground.

Now they were out of the soft, wet mud, but in amongst sharp boulders and heavy scrub growth and twisting vines that reached down to block their progress. "One foot at a time. Don't rush — easy does it."

Through the crosshatch of trees she could see a field. She worked her way slowly toward it, pulling the black horse behind. She considered tying him to a tree and going on alone to find help, but she couldn't get herself to leave him. She was chilled to the bone. Her chest hurt where she had bruised it during their mad scramble back there in the swamp. And her head felt as if there were someone inside pounding to get out. Exhaustion held them to a snail's pace, dragging them down, forcing them to rest frequently. When they finally reached the field a heavy three-strand barbed-wire fence barricaded their way. Three black Angus heifers stood in the middle of the pasture watching them curiously.

Vicki turned left along the fence — groping her way —

feeling for a possible break in the wire — tugging at Pat to stay close. The three heifers trotted forward to follow along the opposite side of the fence. In places where the trees and vines closed in too tightly she had to back-track and try again somewhere else. The black horse had complete faith in her — did everything she asked. But he refused to go on when the wire fence slanted left toward the swamp.

That settled it, she would have to make her own opening. Back they went along the wire. It seemed as though they had been here forever. Soon darkness would be upon them.

At last she found a loose-middle strand in the fence. If she could hold it down with her foot, then perhaps she could break the rusty upper strand by working it back and forth with her hands. The black Angus stepped closer to watch.

By five-thirty the Jordans began to worry. Vicki was an hour late. There had been plenty of time for her to get home, but as yet there was no sign of her. Mr. Jordan called the Hughes, who lived on Bloomerside Road, to ask if they had seen Vicki pass. They hadn't. Bette Jordan was preparing dinner, silent and intent on her work. Wayne stood at the window gazing down Dingle Ridge. Mr. Jordan slipped on his leather jacket and walked to the barn, though he had already fed the livestock. He stood uncertainly on the edge of the road. It was drizzling. Abruptly he turned and hastened back up to the house. He opened the front door and without entering shouted, "Hey Wayne, let's go out and find her!"

The automobile headlights picked out the horse and rider limping toward them along the shoulder of Bloomerside Road. Mr. Jordan knew immediately it was Vicki by the way she sat. Beyond that she was unrecognizable. Black mud enveloped her like a cocoon although it was beginning to crust and flake off the horse. Pat came to a halt as the car stopped in front of him and Mr. Jordan got out. He reached up and lifted Vicki from the saddle, then set her down gently in the front seat.

"Wayne, will you get Pat on back to the barn?"

"Sure, Dad, don't you worry about him."

In the glow from the dashboard Vicki's mud-streaked face looked gray. Her teeth were chattering but she managed a smile as her dad bundled the car robe about her.

Mrs. Jordan helped Vicki pull off her muddy clothes, got her into a hot tub and into bed as soon as they got home. She brought her some hot soup but Vicki was too tired to eat. Propped up on a pillow, she related the nightmare of the swamp and how finally she had made a large enough opening in the barbed wire fence to lead Pat through.

Her eyes were drowning in tears when she finished. She couldn't bear to look at her father. She had betrayed his confidence in her — now he would never let her ride the black horse again.

"Dad," she choked. "I messed up Pat — please don't hate me."

"I don't hate you, sweetheart." Dan Jordan leaned forward and kissed her wet cheek. "I love you."

He turned and left the room, thinking, "she'll be all right in the morning."

When Bette Jordan looked in at eleven o'clock that night, Vicki was bathed in sweat and mumbling incoherently about Pat and black Angus cows.

It was almost midnight when Dr. Plessett arrived. Vicki's temperature was one hundred and four.

"She's a pretty sick girl," he said softly. "I don't know how much is flu and how much is sheer exhaustion — we'll have to wait and see."

13. Recovery

The fever and extreme weakness that followed kept Vicki in bed. The Jordans moved quietly about the house. Even the ducks and geese became less noisy, but only because Wayne got down to the barn and fed them before they could march up to the house and raise their mealtime clamor. He also took over the care of Pat. The horse didn't catch cold but the incident at the swamp had sapped his strength and added to his already poor condition. Wayne faithfully doctored his cut knees to keep the swelling down.

Pat and Vicki recovered at the same rate. While she was sitting up in bed trying to catch up on homework which Kathy brought over every day, Pat started to take a little interest in the pasture. But his old sharpness was gone — he moved about the field like a sleepwalker.

From her window, Vicki could see him standing in the corner of the pasture gazing sadly down Dingle Ridge — perhaps missing her, perhaps wondering if he would ever see Jesse again.

One week after she was put to bed Vicki appeared in the kitchen dressed for the outdoors.

"And where do you think you're going, young lady?" Her mother was setting the table for dinner.

"I'm going down to see Pat," she answered.

"You're going back to bed, dear. You're not well enough to get up yet."

"But Mom, I am well enough. I've been in bed too long."

Suddenly the room began rocking. The color drained from Vicki's face and she reached out, clutching the edge of the sink for support. Mrs. Jordan caught her about the waist before she toppled.

"Wayne!" she cried. "Help me — quickly!"

Vicki's knees sagged as Wayne lifted her in his arms and carried her back up to her room.

When she opened her eyes, her mother was sitting on the edge of her bed anxiously watching her face.

Wayne stood by nervously. "Gosh, Sis, don't do things like that — you scared the daylights out of us."

Vicki smiled. "I'm sorry, Mom." Her voice sounded thin and far off. "I guess I didn't know how weak I was."

Almost three weeks after the "swamp," Vicki walked down to the barn. She felt as if she hadn't been there for a hundred years. The ducks quacked softly as she strolled between them. She stopped and scratched Teddy's lumpy head. As the days grew cooler, his face grew furrier. The bantams fluttered about like quail.

Vicki gazed up at the white clouds and blue sky, squinting into the sun and breathing deeply of the barn-yard smells and the scent of burning leaves.

Pat was standing at the barway of his paddock. His nostrils trembled as she walked up to him. He still looked poorly, but it felt great to Vicki to put her arms about his warm neck.

"I won't give up," she whispered into his ear. "I'll find Jesse for you yet — I promise you."

The day after Thanksgiving winter zoomed down on Random Farm. It snowed heavily for two days. This was followed by severe cold and more snow a week later. By Christmas it seemed as if the ground had always been covered with white.

- The "bucket brigade" went into action. Every winter when the faucet at the barn froze, Vicki and Wayne lugged fresh buckets of water to the livestock and fowl.

This relay went on every day, morning and night — sometimes through waist-deep drifts of snow that clogged the gateways and blocked the entrances to the shelters. The winter was hard on everyone. Vicki felt sorry for Teddy whose beard hung straight down from his chin as hard as an icicle.

Except for brief intervals of not-so-cold weather, the freeze went on through January and February. It seemed as though it would never end. Mr. Jordan rode Pat on weekends if the weather permitted. The rest of the time, Pat was turned out in the pasture for a short time every day. Usually in the winter his coat was clipped to keep him from overheating in the hunting field and when not in work he was heavily blanketed. But this year because he was in no condition to hunt,

Pat's coat was allowed to grow thick to help insulate him against the extreme cold.

He looks like a fat black bear, Vicki thought. But when she ran her hands down his sides she could feel his ribs and the sharpness of his hips.

"Wait till spring comes and that rich green grass starts growing. You'll become sleek and round as a seal again," she told him.

At last in early April the cold released its grip on the countryside. The snow began to melt and soon the concrete-hard ground appeared. Like a miracle, tiny green shoots started poking their heads up through the matted-down brown grass to meet the warming sun.

Slowly the barnyard came to life. The rabbits hopped out of their hutch to bask in the sunshine. The ducks and geese left the shelter of their pen to grub in the mud and raise their racket at the kitchen window.

Vicki was awakened at seven this April morning by the squawking clamor. She leaped out of bed, dressed quickly, and hurried to her chores at the barn. She felt great — spring was here, and today was a teachers' conference, so there was no school. It was Friday, which meant a long weekend; she had finished all her homework on Thursday night, and Kathy was coming over.

The girls had seen little of each other during the winter. The daylight hours were short and the homework assignments long — there never seemed to be time to do anything together. But today they were going to the Fireman's Fair at Mohawk Falls.

14. Country Fair

They left the house in the station wagon shortly after lunch. Wayne was behind the wheel. He had the day off too and had decided the girls needed an escort. He hadn't been to a fair in a long time and he was anxious to show off his prowess at the games of skill. At the corner of Hardscrabble they passed Tommy Rodgers on horseback.

"Tommy's horse is sure an eye filler," commented Vicki. "Look at the way he moves, Kathy — without effort — straight, smooth, like silk. But he isn't as good as Pat."

To Vicki, the most wonderful horse in the world wouldn't be as good as Pat.

Kathy sang out, with a twinkle in her eye, "You can have the horse, I'll take the rider."

Wayne snorted in disgust and stepped on the gas.

Around the next bend the fairgrounds loomed up like something out of a fairy tale. The small field was surrounded by canvas-covered booths. Lines of banners —

red, gold, purple — fluttering like a thousand tropical birds. In the center was a small roller coaster and a loop-the-loop, and, towering high above all, a beautiful red Ferris wheel turned slowly in the dazzling sunshine.

They parked in a meadow adjoining the fairgrounds. The smell of peanuts and popcorn permeated the air, but the sizzling hot dogs smelled best of all. Vicki felt as if she could eat six right now.

Wayne bought cotton candy for all. They meandered slowly ahead, eating the pink sticky stuff that dissolved in their mouths too quickly.

The booths alongside displayed handicrafts and intricate quilting and lovely colorful arrangements of spring flowers.

"Hi, Susie!" — "Hi, Donald!." — Hi, Al!" — "Millie — Frank!" — everyone was here.

Wayne steered them to the shooting gallery.

"Come on, girls, let's warm up here."

He plunked down a quarter and picked up a rifle.

Vicki said, "Kathy, you stay here with Wayne, I'm going over to check the pony rides."

Her friend said she would go with her, but Vicki knew that she really preferred to stay with Wayne.

"Oh no — I'll be back in a minute." And before Kathy could insist, Vicki turned and was quickly lost in the crowd.

She had spotted the pony concession on the far edge of the fairgrounds when they had first driven in. Now she made a beeline for it, barely looking right or left.

A long shed hid the track from her view, but in the foreground stood a low hitching post to which were tied twelve ponies drowsing in the sun. Their backs were toward her and their spotted rumps looked pretty much alike as she came striding up. She came around in front and stopped to scrutinize this gathering of furry creatures. They were pretty much the same height and decked out in western bridles and stock saddles. But what surprised her was that not one, but several of these ponies strongly resembled Jesse. It was a shock that momentarily set her back on her heels, for somehow it had never occurred to her that he looked like so many other ponies. She had always thought that she could pick Jesse out anywhere, but now as she surveyed this line-up, she wasn't so sure.

Now let me see, I'll use the process of elimination, she told herself. These two are brown and white, which leaves ten. This one's spots are too small. Let me see. Oh yes, Jesse had one blue eye — was it the left or the right?

She stepped slowly down alongside the hitching post,

picking up each shaggy forelock to check the color of the eyes.

"Looking for someone?"

Vicki spun about as if she'd been caught stealing and stared up at the largest, fattest man she had ever seen. His huge bulk towered over her like an elephant, dwarf-

ing the ponies standing quietly beside him. His enormous belly, bulging over a silver western belt buckle, was covered by a red flannel shirt. Her eyes climbed upward, following the line of white buttons to his head which blossomed out of his collar like a great rosebud threatening to burst forth into bloom any minute. The clean-shaven face above the rolls of flesh was rather pleasant, with good-humored gray eyes peering down at her. His voice though soft had startled her, but his size held her open-mouthed and speechless.

"Are you looking for someone, little girl?" he repeated.

"Why yes — yes, sir," she stammered. Then, quickly recovering her poise, she added, "Yes, sir, I'm looking for a pony."

The fat man chuckled. "I guess you shouldn't have any trouble finding one around here."

Vicki smiled at his joke, then waited for his face to become serious once more before she continued. "Actually he's not my pony." Then more slowly. "He's my father's horse's pony. I've been looking for him for over eight months now — everywhere I can think of."

The fat man looked perplexed. "You mean that you're looking for your father's horse's pony?"

Vicki nodded vigorously. Somehow she was running out of words. How could she explain her position — clearly — without sounding like an idiot?

The fat man saved the situation.

"OK, go ahead. Look around. I bought this bunch from a dealer a couple of months ago — so I don't think you'll find him here."

Vicki moved away quickly and continued down the line. Here is one with a blue eye! Could this be Jesse? But the next one has a blue eye too — Oh gosh! When she finished her tour of inspection she discovered there were three Shetland ponies with blue eyes. Any one of them might be Jesse. All three had similar markings and all three regarded her in the same friendly fashion. There was one in particular she strongly suspected. He seemed smaller than she remembered Jesse — and thinner. But there was something about him which brushed lightly across her groping memory. "Are you Jesse?" she asked. He eyed her coldly, almost indifferently. Then suddenly he swung his muzzle against her as if trying to tell her something. She stepped back and surveyed all three. How could three ponies look so much alike? She felt like saying, "All right will the real Jesse please step forward?"

Vicki about-faced and walked back to the fat man who was lifting a little boy customer to the back of one of the ponies.

"I'll be back," she said, and hurried off to find Wayne and Kathy. She needed help. Maybe they could remember something about Jesse she had forgotten.

She found them in front of the ring-toss game. Wayne was going strong, pitching with an accuracy that so far had filled Kathy's arms with two black and white pandas and a huge cloth giraffe whose head and neck rose high above her blonde hair.

"I think maybe I've found Jesse!" Vicki burst out.

Kathy turned quickly, and Wayne stopped short in the middle of a windup.

"What do you mean, you think maybe you've found Jesse?"

"Well, I do think maybe I've found him — I really don't know. There are two others there who look just like him."

"Why that's ridiculous — I'd know that scamp anywhere!"

Wayne put down the ring he was holding and paid his money, which the attendant took with a sigh of relief. This boy was much too good with those rings.

Vicki led the way back to the pony concession.

"OK, smart aleck," she chirped to her brother. "Look for yourself."

He did — and Kathy did — then they looked at each other. Wayne scratched his head and grinned.

"Beats me — thought I'd know that pony for sure."

"Wait a second." Kathy had remembered something. "Jesse's blue eye was on the left side. I'm sure of it. I remember when I saw him for the first time, he was trying to reach over the stall door. I was coming in the barn door and could only see the left side of his face and the blue eye."

They quickly rechecked the three ponies. One's blue

eye was on the right, which brought the count to two. The one Vicky suspected of being Jesse was still in the running.

"Pat is the only one who will know for sure!" she announced.

The fat man came toward them. He was surprisingly agile for one so top-heavy.

"Find him yet?"

Wayne took over. "No, sir. Not yet. We think he's one of these two." He motioned toward the suspects. "We're not sure yet. The only one who would know is our horse Pat — and he's at home."

"Would you bring them to our house?" Vicki cut in.

The fat man ran his fingers through his wispy gray hair.

"Well, I don't know. I'd like to help you kids out — but I've got a business here. These ponies are worth two hundred apiece if they're worth a cent."

"Please, mister." Vicki stepped forward. "Please bring them to our farm. I've got a hundred and seventy-five dollars, and I know my father would pay the extra twenty-five if our pony is really here."

The fat man wavered before her tear-filled eyes. He gazed down at the three young people standing so steadily waiting his decision. "Well, I can sure use two hundred dollars — besides, I've got too many ponies anyway. I'll bring both of them over tomorrow morning if you don't live too far away. I've got to get back here before the fair starts at noon."

Wayne gave him their phone number and address, and directions on how to get to Random Farm. Before they left they studied the two ponies once more — without a word. Suddenly they had lost interest in the fair, in the games and rides. Now they wanted to get back home as quickly as possible, deliver the news, and wait for tomorrow.

15. A Dream Comes True

Vicki crouched in her tree, watching Dingle Ridge Road, waiting for the ponies to arrive. She wished Kathy were with her, but her friend had left with her family to visit her grandmother.

The fat man had phoned earlier — he was on his way from the fairgrounds and should be here any minute. Oh, how she wished one of those ponies were Jesse! But that was almost too good to be true. If those two looked so alike, there were probably many others all over the county who resembled Jesse just as closely.

Yesterday when she got home, her mother had taken her to the Granville bank where they withdrew her money. Now her dad carried it for her in his wallet. She could see him in the barnyard, sitting on a bench with Wayne in front of the barn. And far up in the pasture Pat stood quietly, his chest resting against the fence, gazing sadly across the road at the Watkins' sheep grazing in the meadow.

"I'll keep my fingers crossed, Black Horse. Today might be the day."

The truck rumbled around the hairpin turn and honked its horn twice as it approached Random Farm. Vicki scrambled down out of the tree. She heard the screen door slam and saw her mother come around the corner of the house heading for the barnyard. They both got there together as the truck swung up the drive and braked to a halt with its rear end facing the barn.

Mr. Kasper, the fat man, climbed out and unbolted the tail gate and, with Wayne and Mr. Jordan to help, lowered it to the ground. Within the dark interior, Vicki could see two ponies with lowered heads tied to the side walls.

Her heart was pounding so hard she could hardly breathe. Mr. Kasper disappeared inside and came out with a Shetland in tow. He handed the shank to Mr. Jordan and returned for the other.

This time the pony came out first. His head was high, pulling against Mr. Kasper's restraining hand. His forelock was thrown to one side exposing his blue eye. He stopped halfway down the ramp to survey the barnyard and the people standing about. His nostrils flared, his mouth opened, and suddenly from within his small body a rumble began which quickly gained volume and roared forth in such a hoarse bellowing whinny that the chickens and ducks and geese froze in their tracks with heads raised. Teddy the goat almost fell over backwards and Rosalie, watching from behind a bush, turned and hightailed it back to the house as fast as her little cat feet could carry her.

From the upper pasture a shrill whinny answered, followed by the drumming of hoofs. Around the turn in the field, Pat burst into view. His mane and tail were streaming straight out behind and great clods of ripped-up earth followed him as he thundered toward them at full gallop.

The Jordans and Mr. Kasper gaped as the black horse approached the four-foot rail fence. He came on like an express train, then barely checking his speed, sailed over it as if he did it every day.

The pony with a quick lunge jerked out of Mr. Kasper's hand and rushed in to meet the black horse. Pat slid to a halt like a ball player coming into home plate, then stood stock still with his neck arched forward and his ears so alert they almost touched. The pony had stopped too — became a statue, poised, ready to come alive. Pat stepped forward and circled the Shetland, sniffing him all over with loud snorting noises. Outside of that there wasn't a sound in the barnyard. Suddenly, with a shrill high-pitched whinny, Pat wheeled and took off again with the pony close at his heels. They zoomed around the barnyard scattering the fowl and tearing up hunks of sod as they banked their turns. Around and around they went, bucking and squealing like a couple of wild broncs.

Vicki rushed forward and dropped the barway to the pasture. The instant the rail fell, Pat saw the opening and shot through, the pony right on his tail. They crossed the field at a dead run, then pulled up sharply and reared, making mock passes at each other with hoofs and teeth. They separated and "attacked" again and again, each time with diminishing "fury." Finally they stopped with heads raised, blowing. Then the pony dropped his muzzle to graze and after a bit Pat followed suit.

"Well," said Mr. Jordan, "that's Jesse all right, no doubt about it."

Everyone was still transfixed by the sight they had just witnessed.

Mr. Jordan addressed the fat man. "How much do I owe you?" he asked simply.

"Two hundred will do it," answered Mr. Kasper.

Mr. Jordan counted out Vicki's money — and added his own twenty-five.

"Cheap at the price." He smiled as he handed the cash to Mr. Kasper and the rope of the other Shetland he was still holding.

As the truck drove off, Mr. Jordan approached Vicki. She had replaced the barway and was leaning on it, gazing radiantly at the reunion. She looked up at her father.

"Oh, Dad, it's so wonderful to see them together again."

She sighed and glanced around at her family.

"Well, I'll be cleaning tack at the Broads' this afternoon. In a couple of years I should have enough money saved to try again. Maybe next time I'll make it."

"You already did make it," her dad said casually as he filled his pipe. He winked at his wife and Wayne who were both smiling down at her as if they harbored some great, wonderful secret.

"I'm giving Pat to you."

Vicki thought she heard her dad say he was giving Pat to her.

"Giving Pat to me?" Even repeating the words couldn't make her believe it.

"Yes, honey, that's right. I'm giving Pat to you — he's your horse now."

"Oh no, you don't know what you're saying. He's so wonderful — and he's yours."

Mr. Jordan put his hand on her head.

"But he belongs to you. Way down deep inside, he has always belonged to you, I've known it for a long time."

He smiled at his wife and son. "We've known it all along, haven't we? I'm just making it official now, that's all."

"But what about you? I can't take him away from you, Daddy."

"Don't worry about me. I think it's about time we were a two-horse family anyway."

Vicki threw her arms around her father's waist and squeezed so hard he thought he heard a rib pop. She broke away and ducked under the barway and ran like a deer across the meadow toward Pat.

Bette Jordan took her husband's hand. She couldn't trust her voice to speak.

Rocky came trotting out of the woods. He headed

straight for the barnyard but when he saw the pony in the pasture he changed his direction to investigate. Jesse raised his head from the grass and as they sniffed noses, Rocky's tail began wagging harder and harder.

Nearby, Vicki and Pat were standing close together, a single silhouette in a field of sunshine.